THE HEADLESS MONK

Look for more
Sherlock Holmes' Tales of Terror
by Kel Richards

#1 The Curse of the Pharaohs
#2 The Headless Monk
#3 The Vampire Serpent

Books for Teenagers

The Ben Bartholomew Mysteries
The Case of the Vanishing Corpse
The Case of the Damascus Dagger
The Case of the Dead Certainty
The Case of the Secret Assassin

The Mark Roman Mysteries
The Second Death
The Third Bloodstain

Non-series Thrillers
Moonlight Shadows
Death in Egypt
An Outbreak of Darkness

Children's Books
Father Koala's Nursery Rhymes
Father Koala's Fables

SHERLOCK HOLMES' TALES OF TERROR

THE HEADLESS MONK

Kel Richards

Based on characters created by
Sir Arthur Conan Doyle

BEACON BOOK

A Beacon Book

First published in Australia in 1997 by
Beacon Communications Pty Ltd
PO Box 1317, Lane Cove NSW 2066

Copyright © Beacon Communications 1997

This book is copyright. Apart from any fair dealing for the purposes of private study, research, criticism or review permitted under the Copyright Act 1968, no part may be stored or reproduced by any process without prior written permission. Enquiries should be made to the publisher.

National Library of Australia
Cataloguing-in-Publication data
I.Doyle, Arthur Conan, Sir, 1859-1930
II. Title (Series: Serlock Holmes' Tales of Terror)
A823.3

ISBN 0 9587020 4 7

Typeset by Beacon Communications, Sydney
Printed in Australia by Australian Print Group

Cover art Philip Cornell
Cover design Graham Wye

For Barbara

THE HEADLESS MONK

1

'A client to see Mr Holmes,' said Mrs Hudson, our landlady.

'Holmes is out at the moment,' I explained.

'I know, Dr Watson, but he insists on waiting.'

'You'd better show him up then.'

I stood in the bow window of our rooms at 221B Baker Street, looking down on the street bathed in autumn sunshine as I waited for the sound of footsteps on the stairs. As the door opened I turned around to greet our visitor. He was a small, solidly built man, with thick black hair and beard. He crossed the room towards me, limping slightly.

'I'm Dr Watson,' I said, advancing towards him, and holding out my hand in greeting.

'My name is Mr Joynton Oakes,' replied the visitor, 'I'm pleased to meet you Dr Watson.'

'I'm afraid Mr Holmes is not here just at the present.'

'So your landlady explained. Have you any idea when he'll return?'

'None at all, I'm afraid.'

'Has he been gone long?'

'All day. He left very early, before I was out of bed.'

'I don't wish to impose upon you, Dr Watson, but my case is a desperate one, and, if you have no objection, I should like to wait here until Mr Holmes returns. I won't be in the way, I promise.'

'Of course. Take a seat. If you have no objections, I'll just get on with my work.'

Despite my offer he found it impossible to sit down, or sit still, for more than a few minutes at a time. He kept rising from his armchair and pacing back and forth like a caged animal. This made it difficult for me to concentrate on the task of writing up my notes of Holmes' recent experiences in Scotland, a case I call *The Curse of the Pharaohs*.

This had gone on for a little over an hour when the door burst open and a disreputable looking tramp bustled in.

'Where is the great detective?' he squawked, in a hideous, high-pitched voice. 'Where is the great Mr Sherlock Holmes?'

'He's not here,' I replied, rising from my chair, 'and if he was, he would most certainly not wish to see you. Be off with you my good man, before I summon a constable.'

'That's no way to greet your best friend,' said the tramp, straightening up, and so adding two feet to his height. As he pulled a false beard off his face he added, 'Why don't you ring for tea, old chap.'

'Holmes! It's you!'

'It is indeed.'

'We have a client who insisted on waiting for you.'

'So I see. But I must clean this muck off my face, and have a hot cup of tea in my hand, before I hear his story.'

So saying he strode briskly to the dressing-table in his bedroom and began removing his disguise.

'And may I ask just exactly what you've been up to?'

'Working on the Limehouse kidnapping case. I have finally tracked down the lair of the fiendish Dr Grimsby Defoe, and I can now hand the matter over to the police.'

Ten minutes later Holmes emerged from his bedroom wearing a purple dressing gown, his hair brushed, and his filthy tramp's clothes discarded. At that moment Mrs Hudson arrived with the tea tray.

While she was pouring the tea I introduced Mr Joynton Oakes to Sherlock Holmes.

'And what is it,' asked Holmes, 'that so troubles a lighthouse keeper as to rush up to London so urgently?'

'But . . . how did you know I'm a lighthouse keeper?'

'You have the unmistakable gait of a sailor—many years of standing on the pitching deck of a ship gives a seaman a way of moving that cannot be mistaken. Your movements, of course, are disrupted by a lame left foot. This injury, I take it, has

3

compelled you to give up the sea as a profession. What jobs are open to ex-sailors? Not many, but lighthouse keeping is one. Your pale skin tells me that you rarely see sunlight, making it easy to deduce your current occupation.'

'You are amazing Mr Holmes. You are quite right, of course. I am the keeper of the Tregarthen Light.'

'Now, please be seated and tell Dr Watson and myself what is troubling you.'

'Perhaps I should explain firstly that I live with my wife, son and daughter on a small island, little more than a rock rising out of the sea. There are two such rocky islands side by side, known as the Two Brothers, off the coast of Cornwall, near the fishing village of Tregarthen. On one of them a lighthouse has been built, and that, Mr Holmes, is where we live. The other is unoccupied, apart from the ruins of a medieval abbey.'

'And how long have you lived there, Mr Oakes?' I asked.

'Almost twenty years, Dr Watson,' he replied. 'It was just on twenty years ago I had the accident to my foot, and, in consequence, lost my position as captain of a whaler. It was my good fortune that the position as keeper of the Tregarthen Light had just fallen vacant, and I took it up immediately. Two years later I married a young widow who lived in the village. Julia Smyth was her name before she consented to become my wife. She had a baby at the time, a delightful infant named Violet. A year after we were married our son, Robert, was born. These past eighteen years have been happy ones, gentlemen, despite the strange hours my job compels me to keep. I have seen Violet and Robert grow up to be fine young people, and, until very recently, my wife has seemed quite happy, raising the children and caring for me.'

'What has happened to alter this?' asked Holmes, leaning back in his armchair, his eyelids half closed.

'Oh, it's awful Mr Holmes, quite beyond belief, but I swear it's true.'

'What is true?'

'The ghost of the headless monk has returned!'

With that the lighthouse keeper dropped his half empty tea cup and collapsed in a heap on the carpet.

2

Quickly I fetched smelling salts from my medical bag, and, after we had lifted the lighthouse keeper onto the sofa, waved the smelling salts under his nose to bring him around.

'You have clearly neglected to eat both breakfast and lunch today,' said Holmes sternly. 'Lack of nourishment, combined with nervous exhaustion, has caused you to faint. Watson, ring for Mrs Hudson, and ask her to bring a plate of hot buttered toast for our client.'

'Certainly, Holmes.' Having done so, I poured out a small glass of brandy for Mr Oakes and helped him to sit up on the sofa.

'I feel so foolish, Mr Holmes,' said Oakes weakly. 'For an old sailor to collapse like that . . .'

'Think nothing of it,' interrupted my friend briskly. 'Rather than apologies I would like to hear the rest of your story. Who is this headless monk? And what evidence do you have of his presence?'

'As to evidence,' said Oakes, taking a sip of the brandy, 'I have the evidence, gentlemen, of my own eyes. The story behind this apparition, however, is rather complicated.'

'Take your time, Mr Oakes,' I said, while checking his pulse.

'I feel fine now doctor,' he insisted, as he resumed his tale. 'As I explained earlier, the lighthouse of which I am keeper is located on one of a pair of small, rocky islands known as the Two Brothers. On our island there is, in a hollow in the middle, just enough soil for my wife to have a kitchen garden, the rest is bare rock. On the coastal side of the island is the stone cottage in which we live, at the other end is the lighthouse itself. Only several hundred yards away, with a deep, rough channel of sea water in between, is the brother island. This is now uninhabited, but early in the twelfth century a monastery was built there by a congregation of Benedictine monks who wished to live in a house of prayer completely cut off from the world.'

He paused while Mrs Hudson entered the room carrying a large plate of hot buttered toast. This our client began to eat greedily. Between mouthfuls, he resumed his story, 'The monastery stood, a group of solid, stone buildings, until 1536.'

'What happened then?' I asked.

'The dissolution of the monasteries, under Henry VIII,' replied Holmes.

'Ah, yes, of course. Carry on, Mr Oakes,' I said.

'When the officers and troops of the king arrived

at the island, to compel the monks to leave, to close and lock all the buildings, and to claim the valuables of the abbey as forfeit to the royal treasury, one hot-headed young monk resisted. He locked himself in the abbey tower and refused to come out. The abbot urged the young man to abandon his useless resistance, but even the abbot's pleas fell on deaf ears. The king's officers responded by ordering the tower entrance to be bricked up, intending that the rebellious young monk should starve to death.'

'Horrible,' I remarked.

'Quite horrible indeed,' agreed the lighthouse keeper, reaching for another piece of toast. 'But he didn't starve to death. Instead, while attempting to climb to his freedom out of a high window, he fell on the sharp rocks below. It appears that his neck struck one particular rock with a sharp, narrow edge. The result was that his head was neatly severed from his body.'

Mr Oakes took another sip of brandy and then said, 'I have seen the rock concerned, Mr Holmes, and I can well believe that the legend is true, for the rock has an edge like a razor.'

'And it is this unfortunate young monk who is said to haunt the ruins of the abbey?'

'Precisely, Mr Holmes! For as long as I have lived at the lighthouse I have been aware of the local superstitions, but, until now, I have not taken them serious. The Cornish are a superstitious folk, and the coast of Cornwall is dotted with strange local legends and beliefs. However, Mr Holmes, I have now seen the ghost of the headless monk with my own eyes!'

'When did this happen?' asked my friend.

'Two nights ago. I rowed my boat across to our neighbouring island, and, carrying a lantern in my hand, explored the ruins of the old abbey.'

'What caused you to do that, Mr Oakes?' enquired Holmes.

'The lights, Mr Holmes—the ghostly lights!'

'What lights?' I asked.

'For some four or five nights in a row there have been strange, spectral lights drifting in and out of the ruins. I have seen them when I have been at work looking after the main lamp in the lighthouse, in the early hours of the morning. Unfortunately, my wife has also seen them. And they have had a devastating effect upon her.'

'What sort of effect?'

'Those lights have terrified her to an extent that has amazed and baffled me. Never a strong woman, she has been prostrated with terror. She weeps and trembles all day, Mr Holmes. My son and stepdaughter have tried to comfort her, but she refuses to be comforted. I would not have thought her an especially superstitious woman, but it turns out that I am wrong. Fear has gripped her, Mr Holmes, and it is destroying her health. That is why, the night before last, I summoned up my courage and set out to investigate the strange, spectral lights for myself.'

Our client's face had gone pale, and his eyes were

wide and staring. 'I waited until the water between the two islands was settled enough to make rowing across a safe undertaking. Wrapped up in an oilskin coat I set out, with a hurricane lantern resting in the floor of the boat, at my feet. I landed on the island, tied the boat up to a convenient rock, and climbed up the narrow steps cut into the cliff that lead up to the ruins. There I searched for half an hour or so. At last I walked around a corner of the ruins of the old tower, and there, right before my very eyes, I saw it Mr Holmes!'

His hands began to tremble violently.

'You mustn't distress yourself, Mr Oakes,' I said, concerned about his medical state. But he was so captured by the tale he was telling that he seemed not to hear my voice.

'It stood no further away from me than you are now, Mr Holmes,' he said in hushed tones. 'It was a figure, dressed in the brown robe of a monk, with the hood of the robe pulled up around the head. I lifted up my lantern, Mr Holmes, and shone it in the spectre's face. But there was no face! None at all! In the yellow light of my lamp I could see nothing but hollow, empty black shadows within that hood. And I knew then that I was looking at the ghost of the headless monk.'

'What did you do, Mr Oakes?' asked Holmes, calmly.

'I'm ashamed to say it, Mr Holmes, but I fled. I gave a cry of terror, turned in my tracks, and fled from that place as quickly as I could. I rowed back to our own island harder and faster than I have ever rowed in my life. When I arrived back at our little cottage my wife insisted on hearing what had happened. I was too shaken to lie to her, and I told her the awful truth. She cried out in terror and collapsed in a dead faint. I have no one else to turn to, Mr Holmes. Can you help me?'

3

'We can help you, and we shall,' Holmes said in a firm voice. 'You must place this matter entirely in my hands, Mr Oakes.'

'Oh, I shall, Mr Holmes, very gladly I shall.'

'It is now getting late—do you intend staying here in London tonight?'

'I dare not, gentlemen. If I hurry I can just catch the last train. My wife, and both my children, can manage to operate the lighthouse in my absence, but I dare not stay away. So, if you gentlemen will excuse me, I will make my departure.'

As the door closed behind Mr Joynton Oakes I turned to my companion and asked, 'What do you make of it, Holmes?'

'I detect great wickedness at work here, Watson—great evil, and dark powers. We will follow our client by the first train in the morning. Oh, and Watson...'

'Yes, Holmes?'

'It would be a good idea for you to bring your

medical bag with you, and your old army revolver.'

'Certainly, if you think they will be useful.'

'I do. Mrs Oakes may be in need of your medical attention, and, as for the revolver, it may have no impact upon ghosts, but I am certain we will find human villains as well as phantoms at work here. And now, let's get an early night—we start first thing in the morning.'

In the chill, early morning air Holmes and I took a handsome cab to Waterloo Station and caught the first train for Cornwall. Later in the day we changed to a local branch line that took us as far as Newlyn. There the line ended, and we had to hire a pony trap to take us down the coast to the small fishing village of Tregarthen.

'I can take you to the top of the cliff,' said the driver of the pony cart, 'but you have to get down to the village on foot.'

'What do you mean, my good man?' I began to protest.

'You'll see when we get there,' said the driver, holding up his hand to silence my protest.

The road followed the top of the cliffs, which plunged away sharply on one side, ending in the roar of crashing waves far below. It was late in the day, and the landscape was soaked with the red glow of sunset when the driver pulled the pony trap to a halt and announced, 'Here we are, gentlemen.'

'Here we are where?' I asked, as Holmes and I descended from the cart, carrying our bags.

'At Tregarthen,' he replied.

'But where? I can't see a building or a person,' I protested, looking around.

'Below you, sir,' explained the driver, 'at the foot of the cliff. You see over there?' He pointed to a spot on the cliff top as he spoke. 'That's the top of the path. You follow that and it will take you down to Tregarthen village.'

We paid off the driver, and set out on the stony path he had indicated to us. It was narrow and steep, winding rapidly downwards as it wove an uneven path around boulders and dips and bulges in the cliff-face. At length, we rounded one last turn, and there before us was a pretty little village of white cottages, packed tightly together along a zigzag path that ran a short distance up the cliff-face.

'Our destination, Watson,' said Holmes, setting down his bag, and pausing to look.

At the foot of the cliff was a broad, flat area of wharf and seawall, with small fishing boats bobbing in the waves at the wooden jetties that thrust out into the water. Facing this was clearly the main street of the village: there was a combined general store and post office, an inn, a small church, and several houses.

The village was in a small cove, sheltered by rocky headlands that thrust their protective arms out into the deep, green waters of the ocean. Beyond the southernmost promontory we could make out a small island, and, on it, the slender, white tower of the lighthouse. The second island Joynton Oakes had mentioned, the twin of the one we could see, was out of sight, perhaps shielded from our view by the headland, or by the lighthouse island itself.

Holmes and I walked into the village and down the main street.

As we were entering the little village of Tregarthen there were events happening elsewhere, of which I learned only later. In the lighthouse keeper's cottage, Joynton Oakes' stepdaughter Violet, an attractive, red-haired girl of twenty-one, was preparing the evening meal.

She left the saucepans bubbling quietly on the stove and walked to the door of her mother's bedroom. Pressing her ear against the door panel she listened carefully. The sobbing that had emanated from the room all day had stopped. She could hear nothing but silence. Slowly she turned the handle, and pushed the door open, expecting to find her mother asleep.

Instead, she saw her mother sitting at her dressing table, dabbing at her eyes with a damp handkerchief and looking, grim-faced, at a photograph she held in her hands. Just then, Mrs Julia Oakes caught sight of her daughter's reflection in the bedroom mirror.

'Violet! What do you think you're doing, creeping up on me like that!' As she spoke she hurriedly thrust the photograph out of sight.

'I wasn't creeping, mother. I thought you might be asleep, and I didn't want to disturb you.'

'A likely story! You've been snooping around, spying on me, and I won't have it. I tell you I just won't stand for it. Now, get out!'

'I'm . . . I'm . . . sorry,' stuttered the girl, adding, as she pulled the door closed, 'dinner will be ready in half an hour.'

Violet Oakes stood in the passageway chewing on her knuckles, her brow furrowed with worry. She had never known her mother to behave in that way before. And whose picture was it that her mother had been so anxious to conceal? There were things happening to her family that Violet did not understand, things that worried her.

She walked out of the door of the cottage, towards the small kitchen garden, breathing in the sea air deeply, trying to clear her confused and crowded mind. Standing on a tall boulder she saw her half-brother Robert. He was a tall, strongly built seventeen-year-old. Of all of them, he seemed the least upset by recent events.

Robert did not notice her approach. He held a brass telescope to his eye, and all his attention was fixed on whatever he was looking at.

'Robert! What are you up to?' snapped Violet, taking out her pent-up feelings on her younger brother.

'I'm just spying on the Abbey,' he replied defensively. 'I thought if I could see some movement there during daylight, it would prove there are people there—not ghosts.'

'And have you seen anything?'

'No. Nothing,' he admitted glumly, jumping down from the boulder.

'Then you can run to the lighthouse and fetch

father—dinner is almost ready.'

As he sprinted away, it occurred to Violet that two members of her family had used the word "spying" in the last ten minutes. It was a word that haunted her. She turned towards the abbey ruins, on the small island just two hundred yards away, across the surging waves. She felt that there were eyes, unseen eyes, in those ruins looking at her—looking at them all. Violet felt as though she was being spied upon constantly. She shivered. It was a most uncomfortable feeling.

4

As Holmes and I stepped into *The Fisherman's Arms* the quiet murmur of conversation came to a halt, and every eye in the place turned upon us. All the men in that bar were dressed alike in thick, woollen, rollneck sweaters, woollen trousers, and long waterproof boots that came almost up to their knees. They were either bareheaded or wore knitted, woollen caps. That uniformity of appearance made Holmes and I stand out. He was dressed in an Inverness cape and deerstalker hat, while I wore a heavy greatcoat over my suit, and a bowler hat.

'Good evening,' said Holmes, nodding towards the publican behind the bar.

'Evening,' was the reply—more a snarl, than a welcome.

'We're looking to hire a boat to take us across to the lighthouse,' said Holmes. 'Would one of you gentlemen be prepared to oblige?'

At this all the faces turned away again, and the

men stared down into their tankards of ale.

'We don't get many visitors here,' growled the publican, 'and when they come—they ain't all that popular.'

Holmes said nothing, but walked over to the bar, dipped into his pocket, and pulled out a gold sovereign. He let the coin fall with a noisy rattle onto the bar counter.

'One gold sovereign immediately,' said Sherlock Holmes, 'and a second when we reach the island safely.'

There was a long silence, and then a young voice said abruptly, 'I'll take it. I need the money, even if no one else does.' The speaker was standing at the bar, not far from Holmes, and as he spoke his hand shot out and grabbed the gold coin.

'My name is King—Bert King, and I'm pleased to be of service to you.'

'Excellent,' said Holmes. 'Let's be off then, shall we? My name, by the way is Sherlock Holmes, and this is my friend Dr Watson.'

'Sherlock Holmes?' cried the publican. 'Why didn't you say so? We've heard of you Mr Holmes and we're right proud to have you visit us. I mean to say, you don't count as no ordinary visitor. You're more than welcome among us, Mr Holmes.'

'It's very kind of you to say so. Very kind indeed.'

'Why are you here, Mr Holmes?' called out a craggy faced man from a table near the far wall. 'What brings you to these parts?'

'It's the ghost, ain't it?' said another fisherman in

a low voice. 'You've come about the ghost of the headless monk, haven't you, Mr Holmes.'

'I have indeed,' replied Holmes. 'It is, as you correctly surmise, your local mystery that has drawn me here.'

There were nods and smiles around the room in response to this. They seemed to regard it as a great honour that the legendary detective would interest himself in their local mystery.

'Has anyone here seen it?' asked Holmes. 'Even caught a glimpse of it?'

A long silence greeted this question.

'Not actually seen it,' said a voice from a corner of the room, eventually. 'But I saw the light once.'

'When was this?'

'Less than a week ago. The day we had that big storm in the afternoon, remember?' said the speaker, appealing to the rest of the room.

'Aye, that would be six days back, that would,' agreed the craggy faced man. 'Young Selwyn came back late that day, because of the storm.'

'That's right!' said the man in the corner, who we now knew to be 'young Selwyn'. 'All the other boats was in, and I was comin' back late. And I saw a light flickerin' on that island, I did. In amongst them ruins, it was. I hollered out across the water when I saw the light. I thought it might have been one of the fishing boats washed up on the island by the storm. But as soon as I called out, the light disappeared.'

'Revealing,' said Holmes, stroking his long, thin chin. 'Most revealing.'

'My grandfather saw the ghost once,' said the publican. 'Least ways he said he did. Horrible he said it was—glowed in the dark, and moaned fit to chill a man's blood.'

'Your grandfather, George Pendennis, was capable of seeing anything,' laughed Bert King, 'after he'd had a drink or two. He drank too much of his own stock, and that's the truth.'

A general ripple of laughter greeting this announcement, and assured us of its truth.

'Let's be away then,' urged Holmes. 'If we are to reach the island before the last rays of the dying sun disappear.'

'Come along then, Mr Holmes and Dr Watson. My boat's moored at the town jetty.' With these words King led the way to the inn door. Behind us we heard George Pendennis, the publican, shouting, 'You're welcome here any time, Sherlock Holmes. Come back if you want to learn more about the ghost, and about the horrible history of the Two Brothers.'

The evening air was cold, and there was a fresh breeze blowing in from the sea, as we followed the young fisherman down the length of the town jetty, the wooden planks rattling under our feet as we strode swiftly along.

King took our luggage, leading us down a wooden ladder and on board a twenty-foot-long fishing ketch that was moored at the end of the jetty. The young man quickly cast off, and ran up the fore and aft sails. Then, as the vessel began to move, he took his place at the tiller and brought her slowly around the cove and headed towards the island.

'What's the landing place like?' I asked. 'Is it difficult getting ashore?'

'Not at all,' replied King. 'The authorities built a jetty at the island over thirty years ago, so we can sail right up to it. Before that everyone had to row ashore in a dinghy, and climb up the rocks. In those days you could only land twice a day—at low tide.'

Less than half an hour later the ketch was tied up at the island's jetty, and Bert King was lifting out our bags.

'We can manage from here, Mr King. Thank you for your assistance,' Holmes said, as he tossed across another gold sovereign.

'Thank you, Mr Holmes,' replied the young man with grin, as he looked at the sparkle of the coin in this hand. 'Any time I can be of assistance, just let me know.'

Holmes and I made our way up the steps that had been cut into the steep, rocky slope of the island. At the top we found ourselves standing on a small plateau, with the lighthouse at one end, and a stone cottage at the other.

As we stood there getting our bearings, a figure came rushing out of the darkness.

'Is that you, Mr Holmes?' cried Joynton Oakes, his voice heavy with emotion. 'It's my wife, Mr Holmes, it's poor Julia—she's disappeared!'

5

'Where did she disappear from?' asked Holmes urgently.

'From the cottage.'

'Then we shall begin our search there. Lead the way Oakes.'

In a limping run the lighthouse keeper led the way to his cottage. As we stepped through the front door into the small kitchen Oakes introduced us to his children—Violet and Robert.

'She's not at the lighthouse,' said Violet breathlessly.

'Nor anywhere else,' added her brother.

'Where was she last seen?' Holmes asked.

'I saw her in her bedroom about an hour ago,' Violet volunteered.

'Then I shall start there. Bring candles, I shall want plenty of light.'

Holmes followed Violet to the missing woman's bedroom, where he began a rapid but thorough search.

'She left no note?' he asked.

'No,' sobbed the miserable Oakes.

'Most unusual,' muttered Holmes, dropping onto his hands and knees and making a search of the floor.

'Will this help to find her, Mr Holmes?' cried Oaks in anguish.

'You can trust my friend Sherlock Holmes,' I said, patting the man comfortingly on the shoulder.

Leaning forward I saw Holmes scoop up a small piece of crumpled cardboard from the floor. It appeared to be a photograph. He glanced at it briefly, then stuffed it hastily into his pocket.

'That confirms it,' he murmured as he rose to his feet.

'Confirms what, Holmes?' I asked.

'Mr Oakes—if I wished to take my own life, where would I be most likely to go on this island?'

'Mr Holmes, you can't mean . . .' gasped the stricken man.

'To the high rocks, beyond the lighthouse,' replied Robert Oakes, more clear headed than his father.

'Lead the way,' said Holmes, 'and be quick about it.'

Robert was a fit young man and sprinted ahead of us. The lean, athletic Holmes was able to keep up with the youngster's pace, but I was falling behind, with Joynton Oakes and his daughter further back still.

As I reached the cliff top Robert was saying, 'You were right, Mr Holmes. That must be her.'

'How do we get down?' asked the detective.

'There's a narrow path down the cliff face. Follow me.'

As the two turned and hurried away, I leaned forward into the strong sea breeze, and peered over the edge of the cliff—far below, sprawled on a small, shingle beach was a patch of white which could only be the body of Julia Oakes. When her husband and daughter caught up with me I indicated the grim sight below, and hurried to follow in the tracks of Robert Oakes and Sherlock Holmes.

By the time I caught up they were kneeling beside her.

'She's still breathing, Watson,' said Holmes, 'her life undoubtedly saved by the fact that she fell on the shingles, not the rocks.'

I crouched down and felt her pulse—it was steady, but weak. Then I checked for broken bones. She was unconscious, her breathing shallow, and her body temperature low.

'How is she?' puffed Joynton Oakes as he reached us.

'Is she . . . is she . . .?' gasped Violet.

'She's still alive,' I replied. 'And she has been most fortunate—the only broken bone I can find is a cracked rib. But she is suffering badly from exposure. We need to get her back to the cottage and warm her up quickly.'

Half an hour later the injured woman was lying on her own bed. With Violet's help I had cleaned and dressed her many cuts and abrasions, and I was strapping up her ribs.

'Now Violet, she needs to be wrapped up as warmly as possible,' I said as I finished. 'Warm blankets in front of the fire and wrap them around her.'

'Yes, Dr Watson.'

I left Julia Oakes in the care of her daughter and joined the others at the kitchen table.

'How is she?' asked her distressed husband for the tenth time that night.

'In shock,' I replied, 'but out of danger. She'll need close watching for the next twenty-four hours, but I have every hope that she will fully recover.'

'Thank you Dr Watson, and you too Mr Holmes. Oh, why would Julia do something like that?'

'That is a question we shall investigate over the next day or so,' said Holmes quietly.

'She appears to be sleeping peacefully now,' remarked Violet, as she entered the room.

'That's very good, my dear,' I said, 'but you and I are going to have to keep a close eye on her.'

'Oh Dad!' interrupted Robert. 'With all that's happened I forgot to tell you—the man with the false beard was back today. I saw him while you were asleep. And he was around yesterday as well, when you were in London.'

'This sounds interesting,' said Sherlock Holmes. 'You'd better tell me about it.'

'I've only seen him once, Mr Holmes,' explained Joynton Oakes. 'My children have seen him more often than I have. Perhaps they should explain.'

Robert and Violet glanced at each other, and then

Robert began. 'We saw him first five days ago, and he's turned up every day since. He comes in a small ketch. He always comes around the headland from the direction of Newlyn, and departs in the same way. He doesn't sail the boat himself, he has a sailor doing that for him. He just sits in the back, looking around, and spying on us with a brass telescope.'

'You called him "the man with the false beard"—how do you know it's false?'

'On the second day he came,' Violet said, 'there was a strong wind. I saw a gust of wind pull it off his face and blow it into the bottom of the boat. He hastily recovered it and put it back in place.'

'Describe him to me,' instructed Holmes.

'Middle sized,' Robert said slowly, closing his eyes, as if trying to picture the man, 'with dark hair, and, as Violet says, a false beard.'

'He's always dressed in a greatcoat,' added Violet, 'and he usually comes in the middle of the afternoon. He sails around the Two Brothers for an hour or two, and then goes away again.'

'Fascinating,' remarked Holmes thoughtfully, 'absolutely fascinating.'

'And now, Mr Oakes,' said Sherlock Holmes briskly. 'Surely it's time you saw to your lighthouse?'

'Great heavens!' exclaimed the keeper. 'With all that's happened I had forgotten. It's well and truly dark now, I must hurry. Come with me, Mr Holmes—two can do the work quicker than one.'

'Shall I come?' I asked.

'You had better stay with your patient, Watson' said Holmes, as he and Joynton Oakes hurried out into the darkness. What happened next I was only told about later.

Oakes sprinted up the stairs inside the lighthouse tower ahead of Holmes, barely impeded by his limp. As he ran he shouted over his shoulder. 'There are drums of paraffin in the storeroom, Mr Holmes. Can you bring a drum up to the mechanism room—just below the light itself?'

When Holmes arrived with the drum of paraffin

he found Oakes in the lamp room, trimming the wick of a large, paraffin-burning lamp. Oakes lit the wick, and then lowered a fragile tracery of plaster called a "candle" over the wick. As this heated up it began to glow a brilliant white.

'Empty that drum of paraffin into the tank, please Mr Holmes. And then, if you can give me a hand here—each of these crank handles needs to be wound up to its full extent.'

The two men set to work. 'This light above us has a Fresnel lens,' explained Oakes, 'a huge, compound, glass lens made up of triangular prisms that reflect and strengthen the light.' With a touch of pride, he added, 'My lens can project a beam of light over twenty miles to sea. The lens revolves around the lamp by means of a clockwork mechanism. These four crank handles wind up the clockwork. There—that's about done.'

Oakes pulled out a large, red handkerchief and mopped his forehead. 'The light is operating now, Mr Holmes—the ships are safe.'

As the two men sat down to rest from their labours Holmes asked, 'How long has this present lamp been in operation?'

'It was first installed in 1855. But, of course, it had to be re-installed twenty years ago—just before I arrived—after the wreckers had hijacked the lighthouse.'

Holmes leaned back in his chair, stretching out his long legs, and placing the tips of fingers together, 'It sounds as though there is a story behind that remark, Mr Oakes.'

'Oh, there is, Mr Holmes. A horrible story.'

'I should like to hear it.'

'Then you shall. Let me just pop up to the lamp room and inspect the light, then I'll tell you the story.'

In the mechanism room, just below the lamp room, was a tiny kitchen. Joynton Oakes lit the small spirit stove and put on a pot of coffee, then he turned to Holmes and told him the story.

'My predecessor was an older man, close to retirement. He had looked after this light for a quarter of a century. He had never had any trouble, and he never expected any. But then a gang from London revived the ancient crime of "wrecking". You've heard of "wrecking", Mr Holmes?'

'I have indeed. The criminals set up a false light, or beacon, to lure ships onto dangerous rocks. Then they plunder the wrecked ships for loot.'

'Exactly, Mr Holmes. Wreckers were not uncommon here in Cornwall two hundred years ago, but it's a crime almost unheard of today. However, this gang had learned of a Royal Navy vessel—a small cutter—that was being sent from Plymouth to Gibraltar carrying 30,000 gold sovereigns in its strong room. The money was to be used to make a payment to the Spanish government, as part of some treaty or other.'

Oakes paused to pour out two cups of coffee, and then he continued. 'They came here just after dark and overpowered the keeper—my predecessor—poor old Captain Rodda. Then they dismantled the lamp and the Fresnel lens, and carried both of them by boat across to the neighbouring island. There they set them up on top of the old tower that is part of the ruined abbey. By shifting the light just that far, instead of warning shipping about the presence of the underwater reef just ahead of us here, they lured ships right on to the reef. Or one particular ship, rather. And as soon as that naval cutter struck the reef, the gang rowed out in a long boat. They overpowered the crew, blew open the strong room with dynamite, and stole the 30,000 gold sovereigns.'

'How many were there in this gang?'

'Originally there were four, but one of them was killed in the raid on the ship.'

'Leaving three men to divide up the loot?'

'Indeed, Mr Holmes. But that's where they made their mistake. Instead of fleeing immediately, they stayed on the island—amongst the ruins of the old abbey. I don't know why, perhaps they were getting drunk celebrating their success. Whatever the reason, they waited too long. When the Royal Navy cutter struck the reef they had fired a distress rocket. This was seen in Tregarthen, and half a dozen fishing boats put to sea. The fishermen reached the wrecked ship, lying on its side on the reef, rescued the crew, and learned what had happened. Then they saw a light in the abbey ruins and headed for the island next to this one. There they came upon the gang and overpowered them. The local fishermen are strong lads, Mr Holmes.'

'I know—I've met some of them.'

'One of the wreckers died in the scuffle. The other two were securely tied up, and taken back to the village. But here is the mystery, Mr Holmes—the fishermen never discovered the stolen gold. Not one single coin was ever discovered, from that day to this. Somehow those wreckers had found a place to hide it on that small, rocky island before the fishermen arrived. Later, when the police arrived, the island was searched thoroughly—but without success. Later still the Navy conducted their own search, and they too failed to find any trace of the gold.'

'What happened to the two remaining members of the gang?'

'They were taken back to the village, like I said. One of them managed to slip out of his bonds and escape. I remember his name, it comes back to me now—Walter Gilbert he was. He stole one of the fishing boats and sailed across the channel to France. He was never found, Mr Holmes—disappeared completely. The other man was handed over to the police, stood trial, and was sentenced to twenty years in Dartmoor Prison.'

'You don't happen to remember his name too, do you Mr Oakes?'

'Leach, I think it was—Henry Leach.'

'Your story interests me greatly, Oakes,' said Sherlock Holmes, taking a sip of his hot coffee. 'First thing tomorrow morning Dr Watson and I shall borrow your rowing boat, and visit that ill-omened island. We shall explore the abbey ruins for ourselves.'

Joynton Oakes chuckled, 'You won't find the gold, Mr Holmes. Not after all this time, and not after everyone else has failed.'

'Quite possibly you are right. But, Mr Oakes, I suspect that we will find your ghost!'

7

The next morning was chilly, and a fog had drifted in from the sea, cloaking everything in its thick, white mist. Sherlock Holmes and I ate a hot breakfast, cooked by Violet Oakes, and then, after wrapping ourselves in warm clothing, headed for the jetty where Joynton Oakes' rowing boat was tied up.

'We're going to have a problem with navigation in this fog,' I remarked.

'An astute observation, Watson,' Holmes agreed. 'We shall have to exercise great care. However, I had the foresight to borrow a pocket compass from young Robert before leaving the cottage.'

'Oh, I see. Very good, Holmes.'

I sat in the centre of the small, clinker-built rowing boat and slipped the oars into the rowlocks, while Holmes took his seat in the stern, pocket compass in hand, ready to navigate.

It was an eerie morning—the fog suppressed all but the closest sounds. We could hear the gentle lap of the sea water against the sides of our small craft, but beyond that—nothing. Not even the cries of seabirds could be heard. Either they had been driven into their nests by the weather, or their cries were swallowed up by the dense fog.

'We should have cleared the island cliffs now Watson,' said Holmes, his voice sounding unnaturally loud. 'Pull hard on your right oar for a while, and that should put us into the channel between the two islands.'

I said nothing, saving my breath for rowing, and did as Holmes said. The fog was so thick that I had lost all sense of direction. I could see neither the one island behind us, nor the other ahead of us. For all I knew we might have been rowing into the quay at Tregarthen, or out towards the open ocean.

'Now, rest your right oar, and pull hard on the left,' instructed my friend. I did as I was told. 'Straighten up,' he said a moment later, 'and pull straight ahead—evenly with both oars.'

The fog seemed to be closing in even more tightly around us, like a thick, white blanket from which there was no escape. The air was moist and had the peculiar smell that only ocean fog has—like an odd mixture of smoke and salt-spray. Then our boat came to a halt—sliding into a gentle slope of shingle.

'What's this, Holmes?' I gasped, a little out of breath.

'Unless I am much mistaken, our destination, Watson.'

Holmes and I, both wearing knee-high waterproof boots borrowed from Joynton Oakes, leaped out and pulled the small craft up onto the shingles.

'You appear to have found the island, Holmes,' I conceded. 'A remarkable piece of navigation.'

'A pocket compass and a little mental arithmetic did the trick, Watson. Now, let's find the path up this cliff.'

It was the work of but a few moments to find the steps cut into the steep rock, and follow them to a plateau that much resembled the lighthouse island we had come from. I lit the hurricane lantern we had brought with us, and Holmes pulled out from underneath his cape a solid, oak walking stick.

'Since the fog shows no signs of lifting, Watson, we should stay close together. Watch where you put your feet, old chap, the ground could fall away at any moment.'

'Right, Holmes. What are we looking for?'

'The ruined abbey is our destination.'

For the next few minutes we moved forward slowly and cautiously. Soon a dark mass of wall loomed out of the fog. Holmes explored the wall in several directions with his walking stick.

'It crumbles away at a height of about eight feet, and there is no roof or ceiling of any kind. Come along, old fellow, and keep that lantern held high.'

'Certainly, Holmes, certainly.'

We passed through a Gothic archway and soon were surrounded by broken stone walls that disappeared a few feet ahead of us in rolling banks of white sea fog.

Holmes tapped the ground with his stick. We were no longer walking over bare rock, but on square paving stones—as old and weatherworn as the walls around us. Suddenly I heard a low moaning sound that seemed to echo from all sides.

'Holmes! Did you hear that?'

'I certainly did. It seemed to come from over this way.'

'What do you think it is? The ghost?'

'Never speculate on insufficient data, Watson—that is my rule.'

A moment later our movements disturbed a bird that fluttered out of a crevice in the stone wall and flew away—cooing loudly as it did so.

'A pigeon! It was only a pigeon making that noise. But a pigeon is not a sea bird, so what's it doing on this island, Holmes? Could it have become lost in the fog?'

'Possibly, Watson, quite possibly. Hello, what's this?'

'What is it, Holmes?'

'The entrance to some sort of cellar, by the look of it. Quite a narrow entrance. Hand me the lantern, old chap, and wait here while I take a look.'

'If you insist.'

Holmes clambered out of sight, lowering himself into a narrow, black opening. For a while I could see the faint, yellow glow of his lantern, but, eventually, even that vanished. I prowled around and found myself a comfortable, square-cut, rock to sit on while I waited.

The fog showed no signs of lessening. The air was oppressive, the silence total, and visibility almost non-existent. I could have been the last man alive for all I knew—I could see and hear nothing of the world around me. After a while I began to whistle to steady my nerves. Then, growing impatient, I walked back to the black opening into which Holmes had disappeared.

'Holmes!' I knelt down and called into the cellar entrance. 'Holmes! Can you hear me?'

There was no reply. I called a second time, and then a third, still without response. Then I began to worry. Had something happened to Holmes? Had he been attacked? Or simply fallen and injured himself? Should I follow him into the cellar? Or would that just expose both of us to the same danger?

I stood up and walked back a pace or two, trying to think of what might be the best thing to do. I tried to find the rock on which I had been sitting, but it seemed to have disappeared in the fog. Having failed to find the rock, I kept searching and a moment later bumped into a low wall. And there, sitting on top of those large stones, chiselled flat by ancient stonemasons, was a tin plate!

'What on earth does this mean?' I said aloud, startled by my discovery. I picked it up and looked more closely. It was a tin plate containing the remnants of a meal—hardtack biscuit and bully beef, as far as I could tell. I replaced the tin plate on the low wall, and called out in a loud voice, 'I know you're there. You might as well come out and show yourself.'

The only answer was the fog-deadened echo of my own voice.

'I must warn you that I am armed,' I said more loudly. 'Both my friend Mr Sherlock Holmes and myself are armed, so you might as well surrender yourself now.' This was not strictly true, since I carried my old army revolver, but Holmes was armed with only his heavy walking stick.

Still there was no response to my call. I moved back towards the cellar entrance, pulling my revolver from my pocket as I did so, and cocking the hammer. 'This is not a big island,' I shouted, sounding more confident than I felt. 'We'll find you eventually, so you might as well step out now.'

As the echoes of my voice died away, the silence returned—more oppressive and appalling than ever. I stopped for a moment to take stock of my situation. Holmes had disappeared. I had discovered evidence of habitation, so presumably someone else was not too far away. And I could see and hear nothing. An icy chill of fear ran down my spine.

8

While I was lost on the island, wandering among the ruins of the abbey, there were other developments back in the lighthouse keeper's cottage—developments I learned of later.

I had left Violet in charge of her mother. Our patient had spent a restful night, but still needed close supervision. When Julia Oakes regained consciousness during the morning Violet made her a bowl of hot broth. Her mother managed to eat about half of this, and then fell asleep again.

Having cleared the kitchen, Violet took her knitting and sat on a chair at the foot of her mother's bed, to keep an eye on her as she slept.

After a time Julia Oakes began to toss and turn and mumble in her sleep—as though she was having a nightmare. Violet laid down her knitting and sat on the side of the bed, running her hand gently over her mother's feverish brow.

'There, there,' murmur Violet soothingly. 'It's all right. Go back to sleep.'

But her mother's nightmare just seemed to grow worse. Soon she was tossing and turning violently. Her back arched and her limbs became rigid. Mrs Oakes started to cry and sob loudly, and Julia became concerned that her father, who was sleeping in the next room after his night's duty in the lighthouse, would be woken by the noise.

Clearly this was not a normal nightmare—Violet could see that—it was a horrible nightmare of sheer terror. Hot tears were running down Julia's cheeks. Her daughter wiped them away and laid a cloth soaked in cool water on her brow.

Suddenly Julia Oakes sat bolt upright in her bed, and opened her eyes.

'Mother?' cried Violet in alarm. There was no reply. Violet waved her hand in front of her mother's eyes, but there was no response.

'She's still in her nightmare,' Violet muttered to herself. 'It must be like sleepwalking. Her eyes are open but she remains in a deep sleep.'

Just then Mrs Oakes covered her face with both hands and cried out in a loud voice, 'Don't hit me! For heaven's sake, don't hit me again!'

With that outburst she fell back on the bed, and seemed to drop into a deep, restful sleep. The nightmare was gone, and, exhausted by its passage, Julia Oakes slept soundly. Pale faced and frightened, Violet looked at the sleeping figure of her mother. Why had she cried out like that? What phantom from her past had arisen to haunt her? Joynton Oakes was a gentle man who had never raised a finger to his wife—so where had this terror, this fear of physical assault, come from? Violet was puzzled—and frightened.

While this was happening, several hundred metres away, across a channel of deep, green sea water I was standing in the middle of the abbey ruins, blinded by the fog, and cut off from Holmes and from all human help and comfort.

Cautiously I began to pace around the area that was bounded by the low, ruined walls of the medieval abbey. The fog was now drifting in tendrils like wisps of spider web. It seemed to cling to me, and wrap itself around me. As I patrolled I came to a corner of the stone work, turned the corner, and continued my investigation.

At length I came to a level section of low wall. I recognised it at once as the place where I had seen the tin plate with its remnants of food—but now the tin plate was gone, vanished! I ran my fingers over the surface of the wall. It was quite distinctive, and I was certain it was the right place. Where, then was the plate? Who had taken it? Had there ever been a real object there at all? Or had it only ever been a phantom, a ghostly relic of some ancient meal in the abbey many centuries before?

But, I reminded myself, I had picked up the plate, I had handled it. Is it possible to handle ghostly objects, I wondered, do they have moments when they become solid and can be held by mortal fingers? Whatever the explanation—the plate had now vanished completely.

Perhaps, I thought, this was evidence that Holmes and I were not alone on the island. And that made me think about Holmes again. What had happened to him? Where had he gone? I returned as quickly as I could to the dark hole that gave entrance to the cellar.

'Holmes!' I called again, although I feared the gesture would be futile. 'Holmes! Are you there? Can you hear me?'

For a long while I stood there in the silence, wrapped in the fog just as a corpse is wrapped in a shroud. At length I decided that my best move would be to return to the boat. With this in mind, I began retracing the path that Holmes and I had taken to find the abbey ruins. Without a lantern, and without a walking stick to probe ahead with, through the blinding fog, I made slow and difficult progress.

Finally, after much stumbling over rough ground, I found myself, more by good chance than good navigation, standing at the top of the cliff, not far from the path that led to the shingle beach. I was about to begin my descent when a hand suddenly grasped my shoulder from behind.

I cried out in alarm, as I spun around and struck at the hand.

'Careful Watson, old chap. One false step so close to the cliff top and you'll fall to your death.'

'Holmes!'

'I'm sorry I startled you, old chap.'

'Where the devil have you been, Holmes?'

'There is quite an elaborate underground network

on this island, Watson. From the old abbey cellars it is possible to enter a natural cave system that riddles the island. I have just been exploring that system.'

'I see. Find anything of interest?'

'What I found, I intend to show you. But first, what has happened to you? Why did you decide to return to the boat?'

In as few words as possible I told Holmes about the tin plate—and its disappearance.

'Excellent, Watson!' was his response. 'Another piece to add to our puzzle. Come on now, let me show you these caves.'

Sherlock Holmes took my arm and held up the lantern to lead me back the way he had come. But before either of us could move we heard a sound that turned our blood to ice, and froze our feet to the spot. It was the sound of laughter—the wild laughter of a maniac! Whether it came from a human or a ghostly throat I couldn't tell, but the horrible, ringing madness in that laughter was unmistakable!

'The caves, Watson! That sound is coming from the caves!' cried Sherlock Holmes, 'Follow me!'

For a moment I lost sight of Holmes as he turned and dashed into the fog, then I caught a glimpse of his swirling cape and followed rapidly. He led me into a narrow crevice in the rock, at the end of which was a natural cave. Ducking his head, Holmes disappeared into the darkness of the cave. As I followed him into the gloom, I estimated that we must have been approximately in the middle of the island.

The floor of the cave descended steeply for ten yards or so, and then opened into a large cavern which had a number of natural caves and tunnels opening out from it. Holmes paused, holding the hurricane lantern high over his head. Then it came again—that mad, maniacal laughter. It seemed to echo and roll around us from every direction at once. Holmes closed his eyes and concentrated.

'From this direction, I think, Watson,' he said, pointing with his heavy, oak walking stick. He set off at a swift pace and I followed close behind. Here in the caves the fog was not nearly so thick—just occasional fingers of white mist drifted around us. But the blinding whiteness of the outside world was replaced by a midnight blackness—beyond the faint, yellow circle of light cast by the lantern.

The rock floor beneath our feet was descending steeply again, and soon we could hear the sound of waves. Ahead of me Holmes drew to a halt. As I caught up with him I saw why—we had come to a cave that contained some sort of inlet from the sea, and a deep channel of dark water cut the cave in two.

Holmes held his lantern high and we both looked about.

'Over there, Holmes,' I said. 'There appears to be a narrow ledge that will take us around the water's edge.'

'Yes, you're quite right, Watson. Well done. Here, you take the lantern and lead the way.'

The ledge was narrow and precarious, but five minutes later we were safely on the other side and walking down a broad slope, parallel to the surging channel of dark sea water. A moment later we rounded a bend and saw a light ahead—a jagged opening revealing tossing green waves and white fog. And there, just inside the opening, was a small sailing dinghy.

'This is most interesting, Watson,' whispered Holmes at my side. 'This is something I did not discover on my first exploration of these caves.'

Suddenly the laughter came again—and this time it was quite close to us.

'I'm here!' shrieked the laughing voice, as a man, dressed in grubby clothes stepped out of a dark tunnel mouth. He was an odd looking man, with a tangle of long yellow hair, and a matted, stained beard that hung down to his chest.

'Who are you?' demanded Holmes, stepping forward.

'What do you mean, who am I? I'm Crazy Alex—everyone's heard of Crazy Alex.'

'How do you do, Alex,' Holmes said soothingly. 'I'm Sherlock Holmes, and this is my colleague Dr Watson. We're very pleased to meet you, aren't we, Watson?'

'What? Oh, yes. Very pleased indeed. How do you do.'

'What are you doing here, Alex?' asked Holmes, advancing a few steps closer.

'Doing? Doing? I'm fishing. The rest of them are frightened of this place. Frightened of the ghost. I'm the only one who fishes here any more.'

'And you're not frightened of the ghost?'

'Me? Not at all! I've seen the ghost. Talked to him. He's my friend. He wouldn't harm me.'

'And who does this boat here belong to?' Holmes asked.

'It's mine! And you can't have it! You can't take it away from me!'

'No one will take it away from you, Alex, I

promise you that. So, you sail out here every day from Tregarthen—is that right?'

'Not every day. But most days. I catch fish here. And I talk to my friend, the ghost.'

'Tell me, Alex—what does this ghost of yours look like?'

'Like a holy man.'

'A monk?'

'That's right—a monk. And I'll tell you something else about him—he ain't got no face. I've looked inside the hood of his robe, Mr Sherlock Holmes—and there's nothing there. He ain't got no face.'

At that "Crazy Alex", as he called himself, began to laugh hysterically, turned his back on us, and ran into one of the dark tunnels that surrounded us. I began to follow him, but Holmes seized my arm.

'Let him go, Watson. We've learned what we can from him—for the time being. And I've shown you the cave system I discovered—although not in quite the way I intended. I think it's time we returned to our boat, and made our way back to Mr Joynton Oakes and his family.'

'Can we find our way out, Holmes? This place is quite a maze.'

'It's easier than you may imagine. By my estimate we are not far below the cellar of the old abbey. If we follow the upward sloping tunnels we should reach it fairly quickly. And that will mean avoiding that treacherous ledge around the icy sea water.'

'I'm all in favour of that. I don't fancy plunging

into that freezing cold water. Lead on, Holmes, I'll be right behind you.'

My friend proved to be quite correct. Within a few minutes the upward sloping tunnels had brought us into a large, square paved area that had once been the cellar to the abbey. From this the narrow cellar steps led us up into daylight.

'I never thought I'd be pleased to breathe this damp fog again, Holmes,' I said, as we emerged. 'But I confess to finding it a relief to be out of that claustrophobic darkness.'

'I quite agree with you, Watson. Now, let's find our boat, and return to the lighthouse keeper and his family.'

As we rowed back across the deep channel of dark green sea water that separated the two islands I was feeling relieved to be leaving the abbey ruins behind. If I had known the shocks that the day still held in store for me, and the horrors that the night would bring, I would have felt much less cheerful.

10

As we were rowing back towards the lighthouse, Crazy Alex was squatting on a shelf of rock, chuckling quietly to himself. Suddenly a firm hand clasped his shoulder. Alex gave a small cry of alarm.

'Are they gone?' asked a deep voice, echoing out of the darkness from behind the crazy old fisherman.

'Yes, master,' he replied in a trembling voice, not daring to look around. 'They've gone.'

'Good. Excellent,' rumbled the voice. 'Now, Alex—in case they return, I think you and I should prepare an unpleasant surprise for them.'

'Yes, master. Good, master,' responded Alex, with a wheezy chuckle.

'First, you are to gather all the driftwood you can find around the island, and pile it in the cellar. Then you are to go back to the village, and buy the things I tell you to buy.'

'Yes, master.'

By the time Crazy Alex and his mysterious master

had completed their preparations, Sherlock Holmes and I were sitting down to a hot lunch in the lighthouse keeper's cottage. As we ate I told Joynton Oakes about our adventures of the morning.

'I'm sorry about Crazy Alex,' he said, 'I should have warned you about him. Everyone in Tregarthen knows Alex. What are your plans for the rest of the day?'

'Watson and I will return to the abbey ruins tonight—after midnight,' replied Holmes.

'Will we?' I asked, almost choking on a mouthful. 'Are you sure that's a good idea?'

'Midnight is the time to catch a ghost, Watson—so at midnight we shall return to the ruins.'

'If you say so, Holmes.'

'Good old Watson—always faithful and reliable whatever the situation. There's no one I'd rather have by my side when facing a ghost than you, old chap.'

'Very kind of you to say so, Holmes,' I responded with pleasure.

After lunch I looked in on my patient.

'How is she?' I asked Violet.

'Sleeping for the moment, as you can see, but very agitated when she wakes.'

'I'll prepare a sleeping draught,' I said, and after adding a drop of laudanum to a glass of brandy I explained, 'If she becomes distressed give her this to drink. It will calm her and help her sleep.'

I returned to the kitchen to find Holmes putting on his hat and cape.

'The fog has cleared, Watson, and we are going for a walk to the lighthouse to get some clean ocean air into our lungs. Why don't you join us?'

I put on my hat and greatcoat and joined Holmes and young Robert Oakes on the doorstep of the cottage. Robert had the keys to the lighthouse in his hand, while his father remained seated at the kitchen table, writing up his log for the night before.

As Robert led us up to the lamp room at the top of the lighthouse, he kept chatting the whole time—like a guide leading a tour party.

'As the Fresnel lens is revolving around the lamp,' he explained, 'it causes the beam of light to sweep around the horizon like a searchlight, in a regular, circular pattern. To a ship at sea this has the effect of making the light appear to flash slowly at regular intervals. Every lighthouse around the coast has a different timing and rhythm of flashing. By timing the flashes a captain can tell which lighthouse he is close to. In this way, as well as warning of dangerous rocks and underwater reefs, lighthouses are a navigational guide.'

In the lamp room Holmes and I were careful to admire everything that young Robert showed off with such pride. But, just as he was explaining the glass prisms of the Fresnel lens, he interrupted his monologue with a loud cry, 'There he is! The man with the false beard!'

Robert pointed down to the channel between the Two Brothers. There, sailing slowly through the channel, was a small, two-masted ketch. At the tiller was a sailor, while in the prow of the boat, with a telescope resting across his knees, was a solidly built man with a heavy black beard.

Holmes snatched up a brass telescope that lay on a bench, and closely studied the man in the boat. After a minute he put down the telescope with a chuckle saying, 'It's just as I thought. Robert, would there be such a thing as a megaphone in this lighthouse?'

'Yes, there is Mr Holmes. It's here in case my father needs to hail a vessel. I'll fetch it.'

He ran downstairs, and returned a moment later with the megaphone—shaped like a large brass cone.

Holmes walked out onto the iron balcony that surrounded the lamp room, and, speaking into the mouthpiece at the narrow end of the megaphone, called out, 'Ahoy below there! Ahoy! Come ashore, Inspector. Join us for a cup of coffee.'

As Holmes' voice boomed out of the large end of the megaphone the man in the prow of the ketch looked up in surprise. Then with an angry gesture he tore the black beard from his face, and gave an instruction to the young man sailing the boat.

The ketch turned around and headed towards the jetty below the lighthouse.

'I don't understand, Holmes,' I said. 'Who is that man?'

'That, Watson,' said Holmes with a chuckle, 'is our old friend Inspector Lestrade, from Scotland Yard.'

'Lestrade!' I cried, dumbfounded. 'What's he doing here?'

'I think I know, Watson. And while we're waiting for the good Inspector's arrival, and Robert is lighting the spirit stove and heating the coffee, I'll tell you all about it.'

As we walked down the steep, spiral staircase of the lighthouse Holmes told me the story of the "wreckers" and the gold robbery that had happened twenty years earlier.

'And that's what lies behind Inspector Lestrade's presence here?'

'It is indeed,' said Holmes.

We reached the bottom of the stairs, and opened the lighthouse door to be greeted by Lestrade and his companion from the boat as they walked up from the jetty.

'I confess you gave me a nasty turn a moment ago, Mr Holmes,' said Lestrade. 'And I can't for the life of me understand how you knew it was me. By the way, allow me to introduce Constable Poldark of the Truro county police. He's a fine sailor, and he's been looking after the ketch for me these past six days.'

'Come up to the crew room of the lighthouse,' responded Holmes. 'The coffee should be hot by now, and over a cup you can tell me how close you are to discovering Leach's secret.'

11

'Well, now,' said Inspector Lestrade, 'tell me how you know so much, Mr Holmes.'

'It's simply a matter of logical reasoning and deduction,' replied Sherlock Holmes, as he leaned back in his chair. 'When Joynton Oakes told me about the theft of 30,000 gold sovereigns that occurred twenty years ago, and then added that the only criminal caught, Henry Leach, had been jailed for twenty years, it was obvious that the man was due for release. I take it he is out of jail, Lestrade?'

'Released from Dartmoor two weeks ago, Mr Holmes.'

'Just as I thought. And when Oakes also mentioned that the gold had never been recovered it occurred to me that following Leach and recovering the stolen gold would be a high priority for the police. Therefore, I deduced that the mysterious man with the false beard was either Leach himself, or a policeman keeping watch on the presumed hiding place of the gold coins. However, it couldn't be Leach, because if it was he would have landed to recover the money. Why would he come back day after day, doing nothing except spying on the Two Brothers? Therefore, it must be a police officer. Imagine my delight, Inspector, when I recognised your familiar figure in the boat.'

'I see. As simple as that, was it Mr Holmes? And I suppose you've made other deductions as well.'

'Well, I can tell you that you followed Leach when he left prison, and, that sometime in the last two weeks, he has succeeded in giving you the slip.'

'That's quite true,' said Lestrade, looking puzzled, 'but how can you know?'

'If you had succeeded in following Leach you would still be doing so. The fact that you are keeping watch on the hiding place of the loot, means that the man himself has given you the slip.'

'It sounds so obvious when you explain it, Mr Holmes. And, yes, you are quite correct. We followed Leach for four days after his release from prison. At first he went to stay with his sister in the Whitechapel district in London. He seemed to spend a lot time hanging around the warehouses in the Limehouse district, near the docks. But he must have been aware that we were on to him, because, on the fourth day he gave us the slip—went into a warehouse and never came out again. Later we discovered the place had a secret exit around the side. Since then we haven't seen hide nor hair of him. He hasn't been back to his sister's, and he hasn't been seen at any of his old haunts. So, we thought he was probably heading down here, and that we should be here ahead of him.'

'I have a plan to put to you, Inspector,' said Holmes, putting his coffee mug down on a small table. 'Why don't we join forces? The keeper's cottage seems to have plenty of spare bedrooms—fetch your luggage and join us here. Then we can keep watch on the island together. We can help you with your goal, and you can help us with our ghost. What do you say?'

'Ghost? Did you say "ghost", Mr Holmes?'

'I did indeed. What's your answer, Lestrade?'

'I'm always happy to join forces with you, Mr Holmes, you know that. But I'd like to know a little more about this ghost of yours.'

'And you shall. I'll tell you the whole story as we walk down to the cottage to talk to Mr Joynton Oakes, the keeper of this lighthouse.'

An hour later all the arrangements had been made. Oakes was delighted by the prospect of having a police inspector around the place, and readily agreed to my friend's proposal. Lestrade and Constable Poldark set off in their boat to fetch the Inspector's luggage from the hotel at Newlyn where he had been staying.

Around sunset, just as Inspector Lestrade returned and was unpacking his suitcase in the bedroom assigned to him, I was summoned by Violet Oakes.

'It's mother, Dr Watson,' she said anxiously. 'She seems to be delirious.'

I hurried to the poor woman's bedroom, and, sure enough, she was tossing and turning violently on the bed, moaning and crying out in a most distressed manner.

'There, there, my good woman,' I said, as I sat on the side of the bed and checked her pulse. 'Calm yourself. You are safe and secure in your own room, surrounded by people who love you and are caring for you.'

She appeared not to hear my voice.

'Wally!' she cried out, hot tears streaming down her face, 'Wally! Is that you?'

'My name is Watson,' I said in my most soothing manner, 'John Watson. I'm a doctor, and your husband has asked me to look after you.'

'My husband? Then Wally is here. Bring him to me. I must see Wally.'

'Do you know who she's talking about?' I asked, turning towards Violet.

'I have no idea. We know no one called "Wally", Dr Watson.'

"Hmm. Her pulse is racing, and she's running a very high temperature. She needs to be relieved of this imagined distress that she's going through. Presumably it's some memory from the distant past—nothing that's relevant now. At the moment it's causing her such anxiety that it's slowing down her recovery. Bring me the sleeping draught I prepared earlier, please Violet.'

I helped the patient to sit up in bed, while Violet held the glass to her mother's mouth. She managed to drink most of the brandy and laudanum, and a few minutes later she was deeply asleep. Shortly afterwards her pulse had returned to normal, and her temperature was coming down.

'That appears to have done the trick,' I said. 'Hopefully she'll now sleep right through the night.'

While I was caring for my patient, Robert Oakes was returning from the rocky shore of the island, from an unsuccessful fishing expedition. The last blood-red rays of the dying sun had disappeared, and an inky black, moonless night had settled on the island. A faint trace of silvery light came from the few stars in the sky.

Robert had known the island since childhood, and he could safely clamber over the sharp rocks, even in the coal black darkness. He had come around the headland and was walking towards the cottage when he detected a movement somewhere ahead. He knelt down behind a high rock and watched.

He heard footsteps—soft, stealthy footsteps. And then a dark shadow loomed up ahead—a strangely shaped shadow. Robert's breathing almost stopped when he realised what it was—the black outline of a robed monk! Gripped by terror, Robert rose from his hiding place to run towards the cottage. At the sound of his movement, the monk turned towards him. Young Oakes looked in horror as he saw that inside the monk's cowl where the face should have been, there was no face—there was nothing but empty blackness. The Headless Monk had left the ruined abbey, and had come hunting for them!

12

'He's here! He's here!' shouted Robert Oakes, as he burst into the kitchen where we were gathered around a blazing fire. Violet Oakes, Inspector Lestrade, Holmes and myself were seated at the kitchen table. Joynton Oakes was on duty at the lighthouse.

'Who is here?' demanded Sherlock Holmes.

'Him . . . him . . .' replied Robert, in a strangled gasp. 'The headless monk!'

'I take it this is the ghost you mentioned, Holmes,' growled Lestrade.

'Indeed it is, Inspector. But it's the ruined abbey on the neighbouring island that it is supposed to haunt.'

'He's here now, I tell you,' cried Robert, collapsing into a chair, and still gasping for breath.

'Whereabouts?' asked Violet.

'Near the big boulders. You know the place . . . where I like to fish,' replied her brother. 'That's where I saw it.'

'You've *seen* it?' cried Violet in sudden alarm.

'It was no more than two yards away from me,' insisted Robert.

'Are you quite certain about this, young fellah?' I asked.

'If you don't believe me—come and look!'

'An excellent suggestion,' agreed Holmes. 'Watson, Lestrade—let's do a little ghost hunting.'

As we rose from the table, Violet cried out in alarm, 'You're not going to leave me here alone, are you?'

'Why don't you sit with your mother?' I suggested.

'But . . . but . . . mother is asleep . . . and if the *thing* comes here she won't be able to help me . . . she'll just sleep through it . . .'

'If you're that frightened, young lady,' said Lestrade in a kindly voice, 'then perhaps you'd better come with us.'

We left the cottage a few minutes later with Holmes and Robert Oakes leading the way, followed by Violet and the Inspector, and I brought up the rear. We carried no fewer than three hurricane lanterns between us, and I had my old army revolver in my pocket, just in case.

Robert led us in the direction of the jetty, and then veered along the shoreline towards one end of the island. For several minutes we clambered over large boulders, damp with sea spray, under the dim glitter of starlight. We did not speak, but concentrated on getting over the wild terrain. Our ears were filled by the ghostly sighing of a calm sea, and our eyes by the glimmer of blue starlight on the sharp edges of rocks wet from the spray.

'It was about here,' said Robert, coming to a halt. 'I'd been fishing just a little bit further on. I hadn't caught anything, and I had turned to make my way back when I heard something.'

'What exactly did you hear?' asked Holmes. 'Think carefully.'

'Footsteps. Very soft footsteps. At least, that's what I think I heard. Anyway, I turned around, and then I saw it—silhouetted against the stars it was.'

Holmes and Lestrade lifted their lamps higher, casting yellow pools of light over the rocks. Violet moved a step closer to me. She was shivering, but not from the cold.

'There, there, my dear. You're quite safe as long as you're with us,' I murmured

She looked up at me and smiled bleakly. Holmes advanced a few paces and dropped down on one knee.

'On these hard rocks, and by this poor light, it's impossible to see anything,' he complained. 'But I shall return in the morning and look for traces of this ghost.'

'Ghosts don't leave traces, Mr Holmes,' protested Lestrade.

'Precisely Inspector,' responded my friend. Then he turned to Robert and asked, 'You saw this spectre quite clearly?'

'Quite clearly, Mr Holmes. Well . . . as clearly as starlight will permit.'

'And did it see you?'

'It couldn't have. It had no eyes. The starlight shone right into the hood and there was nothing there—nothing but empty blackness.'

'But it was looking in your direction?'

'Yes . . . yes, I suppose it was,' Robert muttered.

'Then we must return to the cottage with all speed,' urged Holmes, leaping to his feet and striding off at a dangerous pace over the sharp rocks.

'But why, Holmes?' I asked, as I hurried after him.

'The headless monk would have seen Robert, and seen him run off. He would know that Robert's first action would have been to inform us, and we would have done just what we have done—come down here to look for ourselves. Oh, I've been a fool, Watson!'

'What's wrong, Holmes?' I asked, feeling baffled.

'We've left the cottage completely unguarded.'

'Is Mrs Oakes at risk?'

'I very much fear so, old chap,' replied Holmes, breaking into a run as we left the rocks and stepped onto a narrow shingle beach. We sprinted breathlessly, and in silence, along the beach, up the narrow stairs at the head of the jetty, and across the island. Holmes was several paces ahead of me when we reached the cottage.

By the time I was coming through the front door Holmes was already inspecting Julia Oakes' bedroom.

'Too late!' I heard him call out. I ran into the

bedroom. The bed covers had been pulled back, and the bed was empty. The room was deserted.

'The window Watson!' snapped Holmes. I looked up and saw the bedroom window standing wide open, the curtains billowing in the night breeze. Within seconds Holmes was climbing over the window sill in pursuit of the phantom and his victim. I followed as quickly as I could.

The backyard of the cottage was little more than a shelf of rock ending at the edge of a cliff. Holmes hurried to the cliff top and looked down.

'There they are!' he cried, pointing downwards.

I followed his pointing finger and could make out, far below us, a dark, huddled figure climbing, slowly and carefully over the sharp rocks. In his arms he held the white form of the unconscious Julia Oakes.

Instinctively I pulled out my revolver, cocked the hammer, and fired into the air. The loud explosion of the revolver shot echoed through the night air. The dark figure below us hesitated, then stopped and looked upwards. I fired again, this time aiming only a few feet over his head. He laid down his bundle, turned and fled.

'Well done, Watson!' cried Holmes. 'You've frightened him off.'

Without his burden to hinder him the dark figure in its swirling robe ran rapidly over the rocks and quickly disappeared from sight behind a large tumble of boulders.

'Come along Watson,' urged Holmes, 'Follow me.'

With those words he began climbing over the rough boulders and sharp rocks that formed the sloping cliff face. 'We must find out,' he shouted over his shoulder as he descended, 'whether Mrs Oakes is alive or dead.'

13

As we began the climb downwards a clatter of footsteps told us that Inspector Lestrade and Robert and Violet Oakes had caught up with us.

'Mother!' screamed Violet. 'Is she dead? What has happened?'

I glanced back and saw Robert put a comforting arm around his sister's shoulder. She raised her hands to her face and began to sob.

'Hold on Mr Holmes, Dr Watson, I'm coming too,' called out Lestrade, clambering down the rocks behind us.

We had left our lanterns back in the cottage, and were climbing over the damp rocks with only the faint silvery blue of starlight to guide us. It was a difficult, and painfully slow, process. At last we reached the body of Julia Oakes where it lay, sprawled across two boulders. She was cold to the touch, however, a faint but steady pulse was still beating. 'She's alive, Holmes,' I said.

With the aid of Lestrade we lifted her limp form and carried her to the cliff top.

'Has she been hurt?' asked Robert.

'Only a few scratches by the look of it,' I replied, 'but I'll conduct a proper examination inside.'

Half an hour later I was able to report that Mrs Oakes appeared to have suffered no serious injury during her abduction.

'Because of the sleeping draught I gave her earlier,' I explained, 'she slept through the entire ordeal.'

'So much the better,' commented Lestrade. 'But what did that . . . that . . . creature want with her?'

'I have my suspicions, Inspector,' replied Holmes quietly. 'Suspicions I am not ready to share until I have investigated a little further.'

After being reassured of her mother's safety, Violet retired to her room on the verge of collapse from nervous exhaustion. It had been a long and worrying day for her. Robert, however, remained with us as I put the kettle on to make a pot of tea.

'There's no time for that, Watson,' said Sherlock Holmes, as he pulled on his Inverness cape and deerstalker hat. 'We must scour the island looking for some trace of the headless monk.'

'Yes, of course,' I said, reaching for my coat and scarf.

'I'll join you, if you don't mind,' offered Lestrade, 'I'd like to have a close look at this "headless monk".'

'The glass is falling,' said Robert Oakes, as he

tapped a large barometer on the kitchen wall. 'There's a storm coming—a big one by the look of it. If you gentlemen are going outside you should take care. The storms rise very quickly along this coast.'

'Thank you for the warning,' said Holmes. 'You stay here, Master Oakes, and keep an eye on your mother and sister. We will returned as soon as possible.'

With that Holmes opened the door and stepped out into the night, with Lestrade and myself close behind him. As I pulled the front door of the cottage closed behind us I became aware that the storm was already rising, and the gentle breeze of an hour before had become a strong wind carrying salt spray across the whole island.

'Where do we start?' I shouted over the howl of the wind.

'Where the spectre was last seen,' replied Holmes, leading the way around the cottage to the flat shelf of rock at the back. There he clambered over the edge, and began climbing down the rough slope. As I followed I looked down and noticed that the low ocean swell of earlier in the night had been replaced by powerful waves that crashed against the rocks with wild fury, sending white plumes of spray high into the air.

'Is this wise, Mr Holmes?' shouted Inspector Lestrade over my shoulder. 'With a storm rising rapidly, wouldn't we be better advised to do this in the morning?'

'We will search again in the morning,' replied Holmes. 'But in the morning all we may expect to find, at best, are clues as to where the spectre has been. Tonight we may hope to catch the creature himself.'

Before long we reached the spot where we had recovered the unconscious Mrs Oakes. 'When he laid her body down here,' I said, shouting over the noise of the crashing waves, 'he seemed to head in that direction—towards that cluster of boulders.'

'Yes, I agree with you, Watson,' said Holmes, 'so that is where we must start.'

We ducked our heads into the wind and pressed on, feeling our overcoats lashing around us.

Heavy clouds raced across the sky like wild black horses. The moon had risen while we were inside, casting a cold blue light across the storm-lashed landscape. The wind was howling now, and continually increasing in strength.

When we reached the clump of boulders, Holmes got down on his hands and knees and carefully examined the small, sharp rocks near our feet. After a few minutes he gave a cry of triumph.

'Look at this, Watson,' he shouted over the screaming wind, 'our ghost wears a monk's robe made of real cloth.' Clutched in his right hand Holmes was holding a small fragment of rough, dark brown material that had been torn off the corner of the robe by a sharp edge of rock as the headless monk hurried past.

'That's the sort of villain I like,' growled

Inspector Lestrade. 'A villain of flesh and blood—someone I can clap a pair of handcuffs on.'

'We have to catch him first,' said Holmes. 'We must press on.'

He led the way around the pile of boulders as we continued to circle the small island. As the clouds continued to build up, the moonlight that was guiding us kept disappearing for minutes at a time behind thick, black storm clouds.

The waves crashed ever louder and higher, and the buffeting winds slowed our progress. When we reached the shingle beach we found it awash with boiling, angry waves, and had to climb up higher to avoid a soaking. We passed the small jetty where Joynton Oakes' rowing boat was bobbing about like a cork on top of surging waves.

After laboriously climbing over rocks and struggling against the storm we reached the far end of the island, underneath the rising tower of the lighthouse.

'So far, there's no sign of what I'm looking for,' shouting Holmes over the gale-force winds.

'And what's that?' I shouted in reply.

'A boat of some sort. Evidence of how the headless monk reached this island.'

Puffing and gasping for breath, Inspector Lestrade caught up with us. As he did so he looked up, then caught Holmes' sleeve and tugged. He pointed upwards, and both Holmes and I followed his pointing arm.

Then with a shock of chilling horror I realised

what the Inspector was directing our attention to. In the midst of that roaring, deadly storm the lighthouse was dark—the light had gone out!

14

The lithe, energetic figure of Sherlock Holmes immediately sprang to life and he began to climb the narrow path that had been cut into the cliff face. Lestrade and I were not far behind him. As we reached the top the storm broke and a torrent of rain began to thunder down out of the dark sky.

We hurried to the door of the lighthouse only to find it swinging open, and banging with each gust of wind. The interior of the tower was not entirely dark, as the hurricane lanterns, hung at regular intervals to illuminate Joynton Oakes' work, were still burning. All three of us hurried up the spiral staircase.

We found the lighthouse keeper in the mechanism room—lying face down on the floor, blood streaming from a wound on the back of his head. I used my handkerchief to staunch the bleeding, and then turned him over.

'Lestrade,' snapped Holmes, 'see if you can find some brandy.'

A few minutes later the Inspector returned with a stainless steel hip flask. 'This was in the kitchen,' he explained.

I lifted Oakes' head, while Holmes held the flask to his lips. He coughed and then drank some of the liquid. A minute later his eyelids began to flicker open.

'What . . . what . . . happened?' he groaned.

'That's what we were about to ask you,' Holmes replied.

Joynton Oakes tried to sit up, but as he did so he winced with pain, and clutched the back of his head.

'Ow! My head!' he groaned. Then he looked at the bloodstained fingers that had touched his head, and added, 'I remember now. It's coming back to me.'

Just then Lestrade returned with a cushion. 'Here', he suggested, 'prop this under his head.'

'Take your time, Mr Oakes,' said Holmes. 'Who attacked you? Who turned off the light?'

'Is the light out?' wailed Oakes.

I nodded in reply.

'Then it must be lit again,' he urged, 'immediately. In this storm, the lighthouse must not be dark. Get the light working first, then I'll tell you what happened.'

'Follow me, Watson,' said Holmes, and the two of us sprinted up the steps to the lamp room. There we found the Fresnel lens still revolving around the lamp, driven by its clockwork mechanism—but the lamp itself had been extinguished. Holmes opened the casing of the lamp and trimmed the wick while I found a box of wax matches. I lit the lamp and Holmes lowered the delicate tracery of the plaster "candle" into place. This was soon glowing a brilliant white, and the lighthouse was back in business.

We returned to the mechanism room to find Joynton Oakes sitting in a chair, sipping brandy from the hip flask. As the lighthouse keeper told his tale, I fetched a damp cloth from the small kitchen and cleaned his wound.

'It was the headless monk, Mr Holmes,' said the man, his voice trembling with fear. 'I swear it was. I was making my regular round with my oil can—which I do four times every night. There are a lot of moving parts in a lighthouse, and they need oiling regular like. Anyway, I thought I heard a noise on the stairs. So I put down the oil can and went to look, but I could see no one. So I called out, "Is that you Mr Holmes? Dr Watson? Inspector Lestrade?" You see, I thought it might be one of you gentlemen. Of course, there was no reply. So I decided I was mistaken, and I went back to my oiling. A few minutes later, I heard it again—the faint sound of a footstep on the stairs. Again I put down my oil can and went to the head of the stairs. Imagine my horror, gentlemen, when I saw, just a few steps away from me, that nightmarish creature—the headless monk. It was the same figure I had seen in the abbey ruins. The same dark brown monk's robe, the same cowl or hood covering the head, or where the head should be—and the same awful, empty blackness inside the hood. I stifled a scream and turned to run. But I hadn't got more than a few paces when I felt a heavy blow on the back of my head. And that's all I remember. But it really was the headless monk, Mr Holmes—I swear it was.'

'We believe you, Oakes. We caught a glimpse of him ourselves.'

'You did? Then it's not just me? I'm not going mad?'

'You are most certainly not going mad,' Holmes reassured him. 'Who or what this headless monk is, we are yet to discover for certain. Although I believe I know the answer. But he is quite real—and deadly dangerous—you may be quite sure of that, Mr Oakes.'

'That is quite a relief, Mr Holmes. But what is to be done?'

'Dr Watson, Inspector Lestrade and myself will take care of the great evil represented by the headless monk, never you fear,' Sherlock Holmes assured him.

'That's wonderful, Mr Holmes, quite wonderful. But right now I must inspect the lamp, and make sure that all is well.'

As he spoke these words he struggled to rise from his chair.

'Just sit there a moment longer, old chap,' I said, 'while I apply a bandage to your head wound. Once I've done that you can check the light.'

Five minutes later Joynton Oakes, with a heavy white bandage around his head, led the way up to the lamp room. He checked the mechanism driving the Fresnel lens, and the lamp itself. Then, relieved to find all in order, he began to explain the workings of the lamp to Lestrade, boasting like a proud parent. In the middle of his explanation he suddenly stopped and pointed out to sea.

'Look!' he cried. 'A distress rocket! A ship is in trouble.'

We looked out towards the storm lashed sea in time to spot a red arc burning high in the sky. This red glow faded as the rocket fell back into the sea.

'That ship must have struck the reef,' said Oakes as he seized a metal tube and opened a wooden case labelled "signal rockets". Loading one of the rockets into the tube he hurried out onto the wind-lashed balcony that ran around the lamp room at the top of the lighthouse. 'We have to let them know their distress signal has been seen,' he shouted over the howl of the gale as he lit the fuse of the rocket.

A moment later a brilliant green arc lit up the dark sky.

'When they see that they'll launch a lifeboat,' explained Oakes. 'Follow me, gentlemen we must get down to the jetty.'

15

At the foot of the stairs Joynton Oakes grabbed four sets of oilskin coats from a cupboard.

'Put these on gentlemen,' he said, 'if you want to avoid a soaking.'

All four of us hastily pulled on the sort of oilskins and sou'westers that the fishermen wore in bad weather. The lighthouse keeper himself picked up some heavy ropes and a strange looking canister.

Thus equipped, Oakes opened the lighthouse door to be greeted by a powerful gust of wind and rain. With our heads down against the beating storm we struggled across the island. At the point along the cliff top where the wooden ladder rose from the jetty Oakes paused. Here there was a small iron post, set deep into the rock, that I hadn't noticed before. Oakes tied a rope to this post and, once securely anchored, let it drop over the side of the cliff so that it hung right beside the wooden ladder. Then he attached the metal canister to the top of the post, and, protecting the wax match with his cupped hands lit a fuse. A moment later the canister began to burn with a bright green light, like some strange sort of firework.

'That will burn for the next fifteen minutes,' shouted Oakes over the screaming storm. 'That should give them enough time to get a long boat ashore. Now, we're going down to the jetty. Hang on to the rope all the way down, gentlemen, or you'll be blown off by these winds.'

I looked down. In a flash of brilliant blue-white lightning I saw the jagged rocks far below, and I realised that being blown off that ladder would mean certain death.

The next five minutes were nerve-racking in the extreme. Oakes descended first, followed by Holmes and Lestrade, while I brought up the rear. The ladder was set very close to the cliff face and that protected us to some small degree from the worst of those gale-force winds. But the rain was torrential, and icy cold, and if the rope had not been there as a secure handhold I doubt I would have made it to the bottom.

When I reached the foot of the ladder I discovered that the jetty was already half submerged, with heavy waves regularly crashing over it. Unconcerned, Oakes was fastening another of his ropes to an iron ring set into the face of the cliff.

'When the lifeboat arrives,' he shouted out over the gale, 'I'll go out to them along the jetty—tied to this rope. I want you gentlemen to stay here, ready to pull me back if there is trouble.'

Faintly, through the thick wall of rain, I could see the green flare burning on the cliff top above us. With the wind lashing my oilskin around my legs, and the rain stinging my face, I waited with the others, peering out to sea for the first signs of survivors from the shipwreck.

It was Sherlock Holmes who saw them first—his eagle eyes being sharper than anyone else's.

'There they are!' he shouted, pointing as he did so.

A moment later I could see it too—a high-sided lifeboat slowly rounding the point of the island. It was making heavy weather of it. There were two people rowing and two more huddled in the stern. The two rowers were pulling hard on their oars, but every time they made progress, a wave seemed to crash over them, and push them back again.

Despite this they slowly crept closer. As they approached the jetty Oakes lashed himself to the end of the rope that was anchored to the rock.

'Here I go, gentlemen. Wish me luck,' he shouted, then he set off wading through the powerful swell that was surging over the boards of the timber jetty. He reached the far end at about the same time as the lifeboat. He grabbed the small vessel with his hands and pulled it into the jetty. He held it there while the two huddled figures in the stern struggled out. Then, with his arms around them, he started back.

'Take up the slack,' he bellowed. Lestrade and I began pulling on the rope, while Holmes used all of his remarkable wiry strength to struggle, unsecured by a rope, out through the pounding water to grab the survivors and help them back to safety. Soaking wet though they were I could see that they were an older man and woman.

Meanwhile, one of the rowers had used the boat's rope to tie it to the end of the jetty. Then both the rowers climbed out of the boat, and began to struggle towards us, at danger every minute of being swept off the jetty into the angry, foaming sea.

Oakes hurried to help them, and, with the added security of his rope, they made it back to the base of the cliff. I was startled to see that one of the rowers was a woman—a young woman.

Then began the long slow climb to the top for all of us, using the hanging rope as a handhold. Finally all eight of us, four from the island and four from the boat, were safe and sound at the top. And a few minutes later Oakes was leading us through the front door of his cottage.

'Robert! Violet!' he called. 'Shipwreck survivors.'

Robert appeared immediately, and then went to wake his sister. Soon the two of them were bringing out warm blankets and making hot soup.

As the four soaking wet, frozen survivors huddled around the kitchen fire, they introduced themselves. It was the older man, with silver-gray hair, who was the first to speak.

'Thank you. All of you. We owe you our lives. I am Lord Trevalyen. This is my wife, Lady Trevalyen, and our daughter Edith. This other gentleman is Captain Hardcastle who is, or, rather was, the captain of my steam launch *Pendragon*. Although I'm afraid there's not much left of the *Pendragon* now. She's smashed into a thousand pieces on that reef.'

'Were you the only four people on board?' asked Holmes.

'There were only two crew members,' replied Captain Hardcastle, speaking for the first time. 'Both were below decks. The ship went down so quickly I'm afraid both lost their lives. If it wasn't for Miss Edith here taking the other oar of the lifeboat we would all have drowned. I couldn't have managed it by myself.'

'Now,' said Lord Trevalyen, turning towards Holmes, 'perhaps you can tell us, sir, why your face is strangely familiar.'

'Because, sir,' replied my friend, 'my name is Sherlock Holmes.'

16

'Sherlock Holmes?' cried Miss Edith Trevalyen. '*The* Sherlock Holmes?'

'I know of no other,' replied Holmes, making a slight bow towards the young lady.

Strangely enough, Lord Trevalyen seemed irritated by the discovery of my friend's identity. But I didn't have time to think about this for, at that moment, his wife collapsed.

'Daphne! Daphne!' said his Lordship anxiously.

'Step back, sir,' said Holmes, 'and let my colleague Dr Watson take a look at her.'

A moment later I was able to assure them that the lady was suffering only from exposure and exhaustion. I arranged for her to be taken to one of the spare bedrooms where she could be wrapped up warmly. Violet volunteered to nurse her. Oakes told the group of shivering survivors that he had plenty of spare bedrooms, explaining that the cottage had been purpose-built to accommodate shipwrecked sailors.

After Lord Trevalyen, Captain Hardcastle and Edith Trevalyen had been provided with clean clothes and comfortable beds and had retired for the night, Joynton Oakes made coffee for Holmes, Inspector Lestrade and myself.

'An eventful night,' remarked Lestrade. 'I take it you recognised his Lordship, Mr Holmes?'

'I did indeed, Lestrade.'

'Who is he?' asked Oakes.

'He is retired now,' explained Holmes, 'but for many years he was one of the most powerful politicians in this country. For a long period he was Secretary of State for the Navy in a succession of governments.'

'In more recent years he held a diplomatic appointment on the Continent,' added Lestrade.

'I suppose I must be honoured,' responded Oakes, 'to have such man under my roof even though in tragic circumstances.'

Soon after this conversation we all retired for the night.

When I arose early the next morning I was surprised to find Mrs Julia Oakes in the kitchen.

'My dear lady,' I protested, 'are you sure this is wise? Shouldn't you remain in bed?'

'I am much recovered, thank you Dr Watson,' she replied. 'Violet has told me how much you have done for me, and I am grateful. But I am very much better now, thank you. Besides which, we have the survivors of last night's shipwreck to think of. And I must play my part in caring for them.'

Despite her words she did not look entirely well to me. She looked drained and nervous, and from time to time she darted glances at the kitchen window as if half fearful of seeing someone there, staring at her.

'Well, I can't make you stay in bed,' I admitted. 'But if you begin to feel unwell I want you to promise me that you will go and lie down at once.'

'Yes, yes, of course. I promise not to be foolish, Dr Watson. Now, I've begun cooking a hot breakfast. How do you fancy bacon and eggs?'

'Sounds wonderful, Mrs Oakes. Exactly what a man needs after a day like yesterday.'

As I began to eat Holmes joined me, and also accepted Mrs Oakes' offer of a hot breakfast.

'Tell me, Mrs Oakes,' said Holmes as he began to eat, 'what were you doing before you met your present husband?'

'I was a widow,' she explained as she poured our coffee. 'I came to Tregarthen in search of a quiet place to raise my little daughter. Not long afterwards Joynton arrived to take over the lighthouse. We met in the village—and the rest you know.'

'Your husband seems to be a fine man, Mrs Oakes—you are a very fortunate woman,' said Holmes.

'I am indeed, sir. And believe me, I appreciate it.'

'This coffee is delicious, Mrs Oakes,' I said, and then asked, 'What are our plans for the morning. Holmes?'

'We resume our ghost hunting, Watson,' he replied crisply.

'But surely the headless monk has long since fled?'

'I'm certain you're right, Watson. But fled where? And how? That's what I intend to find out. Are you with me, old chap?'

'Absolutely Holmes. Where do we start, and when do we begin?'

'That's my Watson! We begin as soon as we finish breakfast, and the search will start at the water's edge.'

Half an hour later we were climbing down the wooden ladder to the jetty. The storm had blown itself out during the night. The morning sunlight was bleak and the breeze was fresh, but there was no remnant of the fury of the previous night to be seen, apart from tangles of seaweed that had been thrown high up above the water line.

The tide was out and the shingle beach was clear of waves as Holmes and I began our patrol around the perimeter of the island. We clambered over rocks still wet and clammy from the pounding they had taken the night before. Here and there they were draped with strands of seaweed or flecked with patches of ocean foam that had not yet dried.

We hadn't gone far when he heard footsteps behind us and voice raised in a shout, 'Mr Holmes! Dr Watson! Wait for me!' It was Inspector Lestrade. 'Where are you two going?' he puffed when he caught up with us.

'Ghost hunting,' replied Holmes. Then, as he pulled out of his pocket the patch of rough, brown material we had found the night before he added, 'any ghost that wears this sort of robe is a very material sort of ghost. The question is—how does a material ghost get on and off the island?'

'By boat?' suggested Lestrade.

'Watson and I searched most of the coastline last night just as the storm was breaking. There was no sign of a boat.'

'Then how?'

'If you help Watson and me in looking for a cave, you will soon have the answer to your question.'

'A cave, Mr Holmes?'

'Precisely. The entrance may not be large, and it may be partly concealed behind the jumble of boulders and fallen rocks, so three pairs of eyes will serve better than two.'

With that he turned back to the search, with Lestrade and me falling in behind him.

Our progress was slow, as we had to check out every shadow, crack and crevice, and look around and behind every large boulder. I was the one who stumbled across the entrance after an hour of searching. It was high up the slope, well above the high water mark. The entrance was little more than a narrow fissure in the cliff face, but just inside it opened out into a roomy cave.

'Up here Holmes! Lestrade!' I called out, after I made my discovery. 'This may be it.'

When Holmes joined me he pulled out his magnifying glass and closely examined the jagged edges of the rock around the mouth of the opening.

After a short while he held up a brown thread and announced, 'You've done well, Watson—this is where the headless monk fled last night.'

'Do you think he's still inside there, Mr Holmes?' asked Inspector Lestrade. 'Should Dr Watson fetch his revolver before we go in?'

'I think the three of us can deal with whatever we find inside. Are you ready, Watson? Lestrade? Then let's proceed.'

Each of us had to get down on our hands and knees and crawl in through the narrow entrance. Once inside we were able to stand upright. Since I had found the cave, Holmes gave me the honour of going first. After he had joined me, and while we were waiting for Lestrade, he pulled a candle and box of wax matches out of his pocket.

With Lestrade beside us, and the candle sending a flickering yellow light over the dark walls, we began exploring the cave.

17

While we were exploring the cave there were events occurring back at the cottage that I only heard about later.

When Lord Trevalyen woke he dressed in clothes borrowed from Joynton Oakes, and then insisted on being taken, immediately across to the mainland.

'You will understand,' said his lordship, 'that I have urgent matters that must be attended to. Now that the storm has gone, surely this will present no great difficulty.'

'I'm more than happy to try, my lord,' replied Oakes, 'but there may be some little problem . . .'

'Then overcome it, man!' demanded Trevalyen. 'Come along! My wife and daughter can remain here for the time being, while you row me across to that fishing village on the coast.'

With that he stormed out of the cottage, Joynton Oakes limping along at his heels.

'I will if I can, my lord,' called the lighthouse

keeper, 'but there is a possibility that . . .'

'But me no buts, man. Come along!'

Oakes lapsed into silence and followed the long striding footsteps of Lord Trevalyen in the direction of the jetty. They clambered down the ladder from the cliff top, and out on to the small wooden wharf, only to find no sign of either the lighthouse rowing boat, or the lifeboat from Trevalyen's steamer.

'Where are they?' demanded his lordship. 'Both boats can't have disappeared, surely?'

'This is what I feared, my lord,' said Oakes. 'Last night's storm was unusually severe. It was certainly strong enough to sweep away any boat moored at this jetty.'

The lighthouse keeper picked up a frayed end of rope and held it up. 'See. This is the rope that held your lifeboat to the jetty. In the fury of the storm the rope has parted and your boat has been swept away. By now its probably been washed up on the coast somewhere—perhaps miles away.'

'And what about your boat?' insisted Trevalyen. 'Surely you have one, man. You must have a boat.'

'Look at those rocks,' said Oakes by way of reply. 'Those pieces of timber, I'm very much afraid, are all that's left of my little rowing boat. The storm swept it onto the rocks and smashed it to pieces.'

'Hmm. I see what you mean,' grumbled his lordship. 'Well, this is a fine pickle that I'm in. What can be done about it, man? I can't be stuck here. I have urgent business to attend to.'

'The best I can do is run up a flag signal calling

for a boat. One of the fisherman of Tregarthen will come out as soon as they spot the flag.'

'Well, do it then, do it!' urged Trevalyen impatiently.

When the two men climbed back up the wooden ladder to the cliff top they found Captain Hardcastle waiting for them. 'Any sign of the boats?' he asked.

'None,' growled Lord Trevalyen.

'I expected as much,' commented the captain. 'So, my lord, how do we go about doing . . .?'

Trevalyen interrupted him before he could complete the sentence. 'Oakes here is going to run up a flag and call for assistance from the fishing village.'

'I suppose that's all that can be done,' agreed the captain. 'Mind you, there's also . . .'

Once again Trevalyen interrupted, as if fearful that his captain was about to say something the lighthouse keeper should not hear.

'Come along Oakes!' snapped his lordship. 'Where's this flagpole? And where are your signal flags?'

'The flags are in a locker in the lighthouse,' explained Oakes.

'Great Jumping Davy Jones!' exclaimed Captain Hardcastle suddenly. 'Just take a look at that!'

'What? Where?' demanded Trevalyen, turning around and scanning the horizon for an approaching boat.

'There—on the rocks. That's my pet bird. He must have escaped from the *Pendragon* before she sank last night.'

'Is that all?' groaned Trevalyen in obvious disappointment.

Hardcastle gave a peculiar whistle, and then called 'To me! To me!' and a large, dark bird fluttered from its perch on a boulder some yards away to land on his outstretched hand as if it was a trained hunting hawk.

'What is it, Mr Hardcastle?' asked Joynton Oakes.

'It's a cormorant—a Japanese cormorant,' explained the captain. 'I bought it from an old fisherman when I was out in the Far East. It's been trained to catch fish. In fact I've often flown him off the deck of the *Pendragon* and he's come back with a nice fat cod for my breakfast.'

Oakes looked closely at the bird. It had dark plumage, webbed feet, and a long, powerful hooked bill.

'I'm delighted that your bird survived the shipwreck,' said Lord Trevalyen sarcastically, 'but right now our highest priority should be getting that flag signal flying.'

'Yes, my lord,' muttered Oakes. 'I'll do it right away.'

And with those words he hurried towards the lighthouse to break out the signal flags.

While this was happening Sherlock Holmes, Inspector Lestrade and myself were beginning our descent into the interior of the cave into which the headless monk had fled.

As it widened out, it also began sloping downwards steeply, and before long we were walking through a high roofed natural tunnel that was dripping with water. Holmes walked ahead, holding his fluttering candle up high. Lestrade and I followed closely behind, keeping within the dim yellow circle of the candle's light.

Because of the water that dripped from the ceiling and trickled down the walls, we had to be careful not to step into the shallow puddles that lay here and there on the tunnel floor, and not to slip on the wet rocks.

'I say Holmes,' grumbled Lestrade, 'where is the tunnel taking us?'

'Unless I am very much mistaken, Inspector,' replied Holmes, 'we are already underneath the sea bed and walking towards the neighbouring island.'

'So, we should come up in the cave system underneath the abbey ruins?' I asked.

'Precisely, Watson.'

'But how can that be, Holmes? We've seen that one of those caves has an inlet to the sea. If that cave is below sea level, why isn't this tunnel flooded?'

'They are separate cave systems, Watson, with no direct connection. This tunnel opens into a higher cave, above sea level. Hello—what's this ahead?' exclaimed Holmes, stopping abruptly.

Peering into the darkness I could just make out what appeared to be a bundle of old clothes lying against the tunnel wall, at the very edge of the candle's dim circle of light. As we approached it became clear that it was more than a bundle of clothes—it was a body!

Holmes hurried forward the last few steps, then knelt down and rolled over the body. Immediately we saw the grubby old clothes, the tangled yellow hair, and the matted long beard of Crazy Alex.

'He's dead, Watson,' said Holmes, feeling for a pulse, 'there can be no doubt about that. But I wonder how long he's been dead?'

'Let me have a look,' I said, made a quick examination, and then reported, 'Well, rigor mortis has almost left the body. There are just the last traces left.'

'So, how long has he been dead?' asked Lestrade.

'Rigor mortis,' I explained, 'takes anything from four to twelve hours to become complete, and lasts for anything from twenty-four to forty- eight hours. So, at the very least this man has been dead for twenty-eight hours—probably longer because of the severe chill down here.'

But then as I stood to my feet I had a second thought. 'But that's impossible, Holmes!' I exclaimed. 'You and I saw this man alive, less than twenty-four hours ago.'

'Quite right, Watson. What we are looking at is an impossible corpse!'

18

'There's nothing to be done for this poor wretch,' said Sherlock Holmes, 'except to catch his murderer.'

'How can you be sure he was murdered, Mr Holmes?' asked Lestrade.

'Look at his back, Inspector,' said Holmes, rolling over the corpse. 'The knife wound is unmistakable.'

'He was stabbed to death all right,' agreed Lestrade. 'Stabbed in the back.'

'We'll press on,' said Holmes. 'Unless I am very much mistaken, this man's murderer is ahead of us.'

In grim silence we left the body where it lay for the time being, and continued on our way, down that dark and sinister tunnel.

'Why is there so much water leaking into this tunnel, Holmes?' I asked, after we had travelled a little further.

'I've been thinking about that Watson. And I have observed a large number of small cracks in the roof and walls of the tunnel. I believe the water is dripping in because this whole rock structure is basically unsound. Sooner or later the whole thing will collapse.'

Lestrade looked nervously around as he remarked, 'In that case, we should hurry. The sooner we're out of here, the better.'

What the Inspector said made perfect sense to me, and we pushed on at a faster pace. Soon the damp, rock floor beneath our feet began to rise slowly; a few yards further on it rose steeply; and then for the last few yards we were scrambling up a very steep slope.

We emerged into a large, dry cavern that I recognised as one of the caverns Holmes and I had passed through the day before.

'I feel a bit safer now we're out of that tunnel,' declared Lestrade. 'Where to now, Mr Holmes?'

'That, Inspector, is something of a problem. You see this is quite a complex cave system, and we may have to search a large part of it. So perhaps . . . wait a minute—can you hear that sound?'

We all listened intently. There was a faint moaning sound, as of a person in pain.

'Yes, I can hear, Holmes,' I said. 'It seems to be coming from over there.'

We hurried in the direction of the noise, with Holmes in the lead, carrying the candle. Lying on the floor of the cavern, not twenty yards from the entrance to the tunnel, we found a man lying on his side, bound with ropes and badly beaten. He groaned in pain as we approached.

'You're a bit of a mess, old chap,' I said as I knelt beside him to untie the ropes and examine his wounds. 'Look at these bruises and abrasions, Holmes,' I said, as I rolled up my jacket and placed it under the man's head. 'He's been badly beaten. It's almost as if someone has been torturing him.'

'I . . .' groaned the man feebly, 'I . . . I . . . didn't tell him.' Then his eyes closed and his lapsed into unconsciousness.

'What wouldn't he tell?' asked Inspector Lestrade. 'I don't understand any of this.'

'Surely you recognise him,' said Holmes. 'Although I grant you the scratches and bruises make it difficult. This, Inspector, is Henry Leach—the man you were hoping would lead you to the stolen gold.'

'Why, yes—you're quite right, Mr Holmes! This is the man we'd been following since his release from prison two weeks ago. So, he has been down here, after all.'

'And he does know the hiding place of the gold,' Holmes added. 'That's clearly what his torturer was trying to get out of him.'

'And apparently failed,' I remarked. 'But who has been beating him like this?'

'Why, the headless monk, obviously,' said Holmes. 'Now, let's see if we can work out where the gold might be hidden.'

'I can't see how you're going to do that,' muttered Lestrade. 'This man's unconscious.'

'Quite so,' agreed Holmes. 'But he can still tell us

a good deal—without speaking. For a start, look at his hands and tell me what you see.'

'Rust,' replied the Inspector. 'His hands are covered in rust.'

'And what produces rust? How about a combination of iron and salt water? For example, a chain that was hanging in sea water would rust, would it not? Also notice that his sleeves are wet, and if you dampen your finger on his sleeve and then touch your tongue you'll discover it's salt water.'

'The cave with the inlet from the sea!' I exclaimed.

'Precisely, Watson,' said Holmes. 'This way, Inspector—follow us.'

Holmes leaped to his feet and led the way, and a few minutes later we were back in the cave that we had visited the day before—the cave in which we had first met Crazy Alex. Again we found ourselves facing an inlet from the sea, an arm of dark, cold salt water.

'If my deductions are correct there should be a chain,' said Holmes, 'running over the edge of the rock and into the water. It may even begin just under the water's edge. In fact, it most probably does—that would explain why it has not been found these twenty years.'

Holmes rested his candle on a rock shelf and the three of us began probing the water's edge with our hands. It was Lestrade who made the discovery.

'Here it is, Mr Holmes,' he said, adding with a grunt, 'it's attached to something mighty heavy though—I can't pull it up.'

'The three of us together just might,' Holmes said. 'That chain is attached to a chest containing 30,000 golden sovereigns.'

'The money stolen from the navy!' exclaimed Lestrade.

'Exactly, Inspector. Come along now—let's all three of us try together.'

All of us were strong and fit men, but it took half an hour of tiring struggle before we got that chest up to the surface and safely on to a rock shelf. Inspector Lestrade then used a small rock to break open the lock on the chest and threw back the lid.

'Look at that, Mr Holmes!' exclaimed the policeman. 'You'll be the toast of Scotland Yard for having recovered that.'

'You can take all of the credit,' said Holmes, 'I want none of it.'

'That's very generous of you, Mr Holmes.'

'I play the game for its own sake, Lestrade—not for praise or credit.'

We were suddenly startled by the growl of a savage voice behind us. 'Thank you for finding my treasure for me, Mr Sherlock Holmes,' it said.

We all spun around, and found ourselves facing— the headless monk! And everything I had been told was true—there was no face within his hood, only an empty, black shadow.

In his hand he was holding a heavy iron bar that he was raising menacingly.

He advanced towards us, swinging the iron bar. But he had not counted on the lightning reflexes of

Sherlock Holmes. Before he had the bar fully raised again and was ready to strike, Holmes had leaped forward, and seized the wrist that held the weapon. There was a moment of furious struggle, and then the bar clattered onto the rock. A moment later Holmes was holding him securely as Lestrade stepped forward and clapped a pair of handcuffs onto the so-called "ghost".

Then Holmes reached into the shadows of the monk's hood, and withdrew his hand holding a black silk mask—large enough to cover a whole face, with just two small eyeholes to see through.

'There is the "headless monk" we were asked to find, Watson,' said Holmes. 'Gentlemen, allow me to present Walter Gilbert, the other surviving member of the criminal gang that stole those golden sovereigns twenty years ago.'

19

Inspector Lestrade led his handcuffed prisoner back to the large cavern when the beaten man was still lying unconscious. Holmes and I followed.

'Now, Holmes,' I protested, 'I really don't understand just what has been going on here. You really must explain it to me.'

'These two men,' said Sherlock Holmes, 'together with two others carried out a daring and evil scheme twenty years ago—a scheme that involved luring a Royal Navy vessel onto the rocks not far from here, in order to steal 30,000 golden sovereigns from her strong room. This island was used as their base. They returned here with their loot, when they had carried out their scheme. One of their number died during the raid on the ship, so only three of them returned.'

As Holmes spoke the bruised and beaten man lying on the floor groaned and his eyelids flickered open.

'It was Henry Leach here,' continued Holmes, pointing to the injured man on the floor of the cavern, 'who hid the gold without telling any of the other gang members just what he had done. Rather cleverly he hid it under water, and so it went undiscovered during the entire twenty years he spent in prison for his part in the crime. As we have heard, fishermen from the nearby village came to this island and seized the gang. Another of the criminals died during that battle, leaving only these two still alive.

'This man,' said Holmes walking over to the prisoner in the monk's robe and tapping him on the chest, 'escaped. By the way—where did you escape to?'

'America,' replied Gilbert in a sullen voice.

'And why, may I ask, have you returned after all this time?'

'So you don't know everything, do you, Sherlock Holmes?' sneered Gilbert. 'Well, I don't mind telling you. I made quite a bit of money over the years, but during the past twelve months I have had a run of bad luck—and lost it all. That's when I started thinking about the gold I knew was hidden somewhere on this island, and decided to come back for it.'

'But since you wanted your search to be undisturbed you disguised yourself as the local legend, the headless monk—believing that would keep the superstitious locals away.'

'And it did too,' said Gilbert, 'except for a strange old man known as Crazy Alex.'

'I'll come to him in a moment,' said Holmes. 'Meanwhile, as Walter Gilbert here was beginning his search, Henry Leach's prison sentence was coming to an end. Having given Lestrade's men the slip in London he hurried down here. He wouldn't have dared to come into the village by daylight, so I imagine he camped out, and crept into Tregarthen fishing village under cover of darkness.'

'Quite correct,' said the injured man, groaning and rubbing the back of his head. 'I slept in a cave, high in the hills over the village during the day, and came out at night. I wanted to make sure the coast was clear before I approached the island.'

'And what you discovered,' Holmes continued, 'in the conversations you overheard, was that the headless monk had returned. You must have guessed it was someone after the gold. You also learned that Crazy Alex was the only person who ever visited the "haunted island". I think I can guess what happened next. You exploited poor old Alex's distinctive appearance—you purchased a wig and beard at some large nearby town, then one night you attacked old Alex, overpowered him, and took his place. Wearing his clothes, with a long, tangled wig of yellow hair, and a long matted beard, you could easily pass for him. That's what you did, isn't it, Henry Leach?'

'I'm sayin' nothin'. I'm not going to incriminate myself.'

'But why did we find Alex's body in the tunnel?' I asked.

'Because, Watson, Leach here could hardly leave

Alex's body in the village where it would be found. Nor could he throw it into the sea where there would be a risk of it washing up on a nearby beach. His safest course was to bring the body to this island, when he sailed here in Crazy Alex's own boat, and hide it somewhere here. Which is exactly what he did.'

'I think I'm beginning to understand,' said Inspector Lestrade, scratching his head. 'Both the remaining members of the old gang, Henry Leach and Walter Gilbert, ended up on this island at the same time—each determined to get the gold for himself, and each of them in disguise. Gilbert was disguised as the headless monk, and Leach was disguised as Crazy Alex.'

'That's it precisely,' agreed Holmes. 'So you see, Watson, it was this man, not the real Crazy Alex—that we spoke to yesterday.'

'Yes, of course!' I said, 'and that's why the time of Alex's death was so confusing. He was already dead when we were meeting the man we thought was Alex but was really Henry Leach in disguise.'

'Hang on, this is going a bit fast for me,' complained Lestrade.

'Think about it, Inspector,' said Holmes. 'It's really quite simple. But I warn you—there are more loose ends still to be tied up, so I suggest we return to the lighthouse keeper's cottage with our two prisoners, and I'll explain the rest of what's been going on.'

'Good idea, Mr Holmes,' agreed Lestrade.

'Constable Poldark is due in his boat this afternoon—he'll be able to take our prisoners to the cells at Newlyn police station.'

Battered and bruised, Henry Leach was in no condition to resist arrest, and quietly came along with us and we began our return, back down the undersea tunnel through which we had come. Walter Gilbert was clearly boiling with anger, but the handcuffs restrained him.

With only one flickering candle to light our way we made slow progress through the dark, damp tunnel with it constant dripping, trickling streams of water. Just past the half way point we reached the corpse of the real Crazy Alex.

'I think we should leave the body here for the time being,' suggested Lestrade. 'We have our hands full keeping an eye on these two prisoners. I'll send Constable Poldark to recover the body when he arrives this afternoon.'

'Just as you wish, Lestrade,' said Holmes, as we turned to resumed our slow progress through the tunnel. But as we did so we became aware of a light ahead It was the steady yellow glow of a hurricane lantern. Soon Lord Trevalyen and Captain Hardcastle came into view. Trevalyen had a revolver in his hand, while Hardcastle carried the lantern and had a strange looking bird perched on his shoulder.

'Gentlemen! Are we glad to see you!' I exclaimed. 'You can give us a hand with our prisoners.'

'Watson,' snapped Holmes. 'You don't understand. These two are part of the other side of the puzzle. They are in league with these criminals.'

'Quite correct, Mr Sherlock Holmes,' said Lord Trevalyen, raising his revolver and pointing it at Holmes' head.

'But . . . but . . .' I spluttered, 'I don't understand.'

'Ask yourself this,' said Holmes in his usual quiet voice, apparently undisturbed by Trevalyen's revolver, 'how did the gang know that the gold shipment was being made? How did they know which ship was carrying the gold, and when it was sailing? Obviously they had inside knowledge. And when Lord Trevalyen turned up here, so soon after the release of Henry Leach from prison, it occurred to me that such inside knowledge may well have come from the very top.'

'The top, Mr Holmes?' asked Inspector Lestrade, sounding puzzled.

'Twenty years ago, Lestrade,' Holmes explained, 'his lordship here was the Secretary of State for the Navy. He would have known everything about the gold shipment. He is here now for the same reason as Leach and Gilbert—to take the gold for himself.'

'But they were shipwrecked, Mr Holmes,' protested Lestrade.

'That was not part of the plan,' Holmes explained. 'What happened must be something like this. Gilbert saw through Leach's disguise and realised he was not the real Crazy Alex. He tied him up, and tried to make him reveal the location of the gold. This he refused to do, but he did let slip that Lord Trevalyen was on his way down here. Leach and Trevalyen have been working hand in glove from the beginning. Leach was Trevalyen's contact twenty years ago, and he made contact with him again as soon as he was out of prison and had given the police the slip.'

'But the shipwreck—why did that happen?' asked Lestrade.

'With the storm rising,' continued Holmes, 'Gilbert, in his headless monk disguise, went to the lighthouse to extinguish the light in the hope of causing a shipwreck and preventing Trevalyen from arriving. His plan very nearly worked.'

'This is astonishing, Mr Holmes. But everything you say makes sense. It all holds together.'

'You are far too clever for your own good, Mr Holmes,' hissed Lord Trevalyen. 'And for that you, and your friends, must die. Hardcastle—release the bird!'

Captain Hardcastle lifted the large, dark bird from his shoulder, and flung it into the air as he shouted the command 'Kill! Kill!' and pointed at Sherlock Holmes.

The creature flew straight as an arrow, and just as fast, at Holmes, clutched at his shoulder with its feet and drove its powerful, long curved beak into his neck. There was a spurt of blood, and Holmes collapsed.

20

I forgot all about the revolver in Lord Trevalyen's hand and leaped to the aid of my friend and colleague. With both hands I wrenched the bird from Holmes' neck and flung it against the wall of the tunnel. Pulling out a handkerchief I staunched the flow of blood from his wound. Fortunately the bird's razor sharp beak had missed both the jugular vein and the carotid artery. Sherlock Holmes would live.

'Very courageous, Dr Watson,' sneered Lord Trevalyen, 'and very pointless. If Holmes does not die in one manner, he will die in another—as will you all.'

As he spoke he raised his revolver and took aim.

'Don't fire that in here,' snapped Holmes. His voice was weak, but his manner was commanding. The tone of authority in his voice caused Trevalyen to hesitate.

'Can't you see,' continued Holmes, 'that this whole structure is unstable? A gunshot in here could cause this entire tunnel to collapse.'

'Don't believe him,' snarled Captain Hardcastle. 'He's just saying that in a feeble attempt to save his own life.'

'It's an interesting theory you propose, Mr Holmes,' said Lord Trevalyen coldly. 'Let's put it to the test, shall we?' With these words he raised his revolver and pulled the trigger. But at the last moment, just as he was squeezing the trigger, he swung around and pointed the weapon at Walter Gilbert, still dressed in his monk's robe. He was shot straight between the eyes, and dropped dead at our feet, instantly.

'You're a cold-blooded swine, Trevalyen,' growled Inspector Lestrade menacingly, 'and I'll see that you'll pay for this.'

'Not if you're dead, you won't,' responded the murderer.

At the moment there was a sharp crack from somewhere in the darkness of the tunnel behind us, followed by the sound of gushing water.

'The tunnel!' snapped Holmes. 'It's starting to give way.' As he spoke I saw both Hardcastle and Trevalyen staring past me, at some point over my shoulder, as if hypnotised. They appeared to be frozen to the spot, and unable to move.

'Come on!' shouted Holmes, grabbing my arm. 'Run for your life! Don't look back.'

I have learned over the years that when Holmes issues an urgent instruction it is wise to obey it. Without looking back, I ran. As I ran I heard a thunder of roaring water echoing down the tunnel.

The thunder seemed to be gaining. It seemed to be travelling faster than I could run. I ran harder. I was aware of Inspector Lestrade and Henry Leach, both by my side, both running as hard as I was.

It seemed to take an agonising amount of time to reach the tunnel exit on the lighthouse island. Just before I crawled out of the narrow opening I glanced back. A wall of water was thundering towards me, and there, caught up in that wave and being pushed along by it, was Sherlock Holmes with one arm around Trevalyen and the other around Hardcastle.

I stood frozen to the spot. I was at the top of a steep slope that led from the cave entrance, down to the tunnel proper beneath sea level. It was a very steep slope. Like a tidal wave the water came rushing forward. It hit the slope and pushed upwards like a giant wave hitting a beach. It could feel its spray in my face. And then it reached its peak and began to roll backwards, leaving, lying at my feet, Holmes, Hardcastle and Trevalyen like driftwood left on a beach by a storm.

Two hours later Holmes and I were seated in the kitchen of the lighthouse keeper's cottage. We were dressed in warm, dry clothes, and were sipping hot cups of coffee. We had just farewelled Inspector Lestrade and Constable Poldark with their prisoners. Joynton Oakes, together with Violet and Robert, were down at the island's jetty seeing them off. Daphne and her mother were in the upstairs sitting room tearfully consoling each other. They had been shocked to learn of Trevalyen's criminal activities.

There were only three of us in the kitchen—Mrs Julia Oakes, Holmes and myself.

'I must take this opportunity, Mrs Oakes,' said Holmes quietly, 'to assure you that your secret is safe with me.'

'You know then?' she asked, meeting his eyes.

'It wasn't hard to guess. A village as small and remote as Tregarthen is a strange place for a widow to chose in which to raise a small child. That was not why you came here. You came because your husband sent you—perhaps to spy out the land.'

'Husband?' I asked. 'What husband?'

'Walter Gilbert, of the gold robbery gang. He is the "Wally" you cried out for in your feverish nightmare, is he not, Mrs Oakes?' said Holmes gently.

'It's true, Mr Holmes,' sobbed the woman, sitting down at the kitchen table, and dabbing at her eyes with a handkerchief. 'I was Walter Gilbert's wife—Violet is his daughter. As he and the gang made their elaborate plans for the gold robbery I was sent down here to find out everything about the locality that I could for them. I was not part of their criminal schemes, but I was terrified of Walter—he was a violent man, and I had no choice but to do what he told me. And then, the robbery went wrong. When Henry Leach was arrested and Walter fled I felt free of his dark shadow—really free for the first time in a very long time. Then Joynton arrived. Two years later he asked me to marry him. I had heard nothing of Walter for two years and I assumed he was dead.

I accepted Joynton's proposal. I have been very happy with him.'

'But when the headless monk was reported to be on the neighbouring island, you didn't think it was a ghost—you immediately feared that Walter Gilbert had returned to find the hidden gold?'

'That's right, Mr Holmes. The very thought of Walter still being alive destroyed my nerves. I watched the island using my son's telescope. I saw the figure they called "the headless monk", and, from his general size and build, I was convinced it was Walter. I was terrified. Not only for myself, but for Violet as well. Worse than that—I was convinced that he had seen me, and that once he had recovered the gold he would come for me, and for Violet too, and insist that we come away with him.'

'He had seen you,' said Holmes, 'that's why he tried to abduct you on the night of the storm. But he is dead now, and all of that is over.'

'When I was young, Mr Holmes, I was very foolish—very foolish and very frightened. More than that—I did wrong, Mr Holmes, I know I did wrong. It is all old history, and I just wish it could all be buried, forgiven and forgotten. I have tried to be a good wife to Joynton. I never told Joynton about my history—I didn't want to worry or alarm him. Have I done wrong, Mr Holmes?'

'We have all done wrong, Mrs Oakes,' replied Sherlock Holmes. 'The point is, that forgiveness is available—regardless of what we have done. True repentance leads to true forgiveness.'

'We have the good fortune to live in a Christian country,' I added, 'and once a year our nation pauses to celebrate Easter—an annual reminder that God himself, in Jesus Christ, came into our world to pay the awful price that had to be paid to make forgiveness available to us. In dying on that cross, on a hill outside Jerusalem, nineteen hundred years ago, Jesus paid for all the damage we have ever done—for all those years we have spent ignoring God.'

'Thank you, Dr Watson. And, thank you, Mr Holmes, thank you both,' she sobbed.

'Come along, Watson, we must pack our bags and be on our way. There is more work and more crime, waiting for us back in Baker Street.'

Sherlock Holmes and Dr Watson will return in

The Vampire Serpent

Watch for it!

A Note from the desk of Kel Richards

In "The Adventure of the Veiled Lodger" by Sir Arthur Conan Doyle, Dr Watson refers to the story concerning "the politician, the lighthouse, and the trained cormorant", but nowhere does he reveal the details of that story.

This is not unusual, for, although Sherlock Holmes had a career as a detective lasting some 23 years, and, in that time, may have tackled around 2,000 case, Conan Doyle has recorded only 60 of these—in 56 short stories and four short novels.

Of course, Watson's words set my brain ticking over—what could possibly link together a politician, a lighthouse, and a trained cormorant? This story is the answer to that puzzle.

Remember that your suggestions for future Sherlock Holmes adventures are always welcome (the more mysterious and spooky the better!).

Next in this series, Holmes and Watson encounter a villain of almost supernatural powers in the adventure of *The Vampire Serpent*—don't miss it!

Best wishes (and good detecting!),

Kel Richards

SHERLOCK HOLMES' TALES OF TERROR

A preview of what's next from

Kel Richards

THE VAMPIRE SERPENT

1

'Mr Holmes! Dr Watson! Come quickly,' shouted the visitor who burst into our rooms at 221B Baker Street. Holmes and I looked up from our breakfast table to discover that our early morning visitor was the Reverend Henry Bunyan, the vicar of our local parish church, St Bede's of Baker Street. Mr Bunyan was a middle-aged man, portly and affable—a descendant of the famous author of *Pilgrim's Progress*—and something of an expert on folklore.

He stood trembling in our doorway, his face flushed and his manner agitated.

'Come,' said Sherlock Holmes, springing out of his chair. 'Come in and take a seat. Tell us what has happened.'

'There is no time for that, Mr Holmes,' said the clergyman, twisting his broad-brimmed black hat in his hands, 'You must come at once. It's my neighbour, Crosby, the banker. He's dead, Mr Holmes. It's hideous, utterly hideous.'

Without a word Holmes reached for his jacket. As he slipped it on he said, 'Come along, Watson—the game's afoot, and I shall want you at my side.'

As I swallowed a piece of toast and reached for my coat, Mr Bunyan said, 'Oh, yes Dr Watson—your medical knowledge will be needed.'

We followed the bustling, agitated clergyman down our stairs and out into the early morning mist. It was a cold, gray, overcast day. As we walked briskly down the street, Mr Bunyan explained breathlessly, 'Mrs Crosby came to me first thing this morning saying that her husband had not been home all night. He had given her no warning that he would be away, and as he is normally the most considerate and reliable of men, she was deeply alarmed, and asked me what should be done. I proposed searching the bank premises and the surrounding area, which we did. We found poor Crosby—or, rather, what is left of him—in an alley behind the bank.'

By the time Mr Bunyan had completed his explanations we had walked rapidly passed the parish church of St Bede's, and the vicarage next door, and reached the two-storey brick building which consisted of bank offices downstairs, and accommodation for the manager upstairs. Here the morning mist seemed to have accumulated in cold, clammy white tentacles that wrapped themselves around us. Bunyan led us down the narrow pedestrian lane between the vicarage and the bank, and then turned into the even narrower dark alley that ran behind the back wall of the bank building.

Lying against this wall was something covered by a sheet of canvas.

'I covered him up, as you can see,' said Bunyan. 'It seemed the decent thing to do.'

Holmes stepped forward and pulled back the canvas revealing one of the most horrible sights I have ever encountered. It was a dead body all right, but it was a withered and shrunken dead body. The skin was clinging to the bones like dried parchment. The body looked as if it had been sucked dry. The mouth was frozen open in a silent scream of terror.

'Are you certain this is Crosby?' asked Holmes.

'Who else could it be?' replied the vicar. 'Look at that red hair and moustache. And he's wearing the clothes Crosby was wearing when his wife last saw him. But, I grant you the body has been so horribly treated that his face is impossible to recognise.'

'How old was Crosby?'

'In his early forties. He has had a very rapid rise in the bank to have become a manager at such an early age. His wife, or, I should say, his widow, is a great deal younger than himself—she is barely nineteen.'

'This is indeed remarkable,' said Sherlock Holmes as he dropped down on one knee to examine the corpse. 'What do you make of this, Watson?'

I conducted a brief examination. 'Astonishing! There is no blood in this body. It has been drained of every last drop of blood.'

Glancing down the alley, Holmes spotted a street urchin he recognised.

'Wiggins! Come here a moment!'

'Yes, Mr Holmes,' panted the grubby faced little scoundrel as he ran towards us, 'What'd you want?'

'Here's sixpence—run and fetch a policeman. Urgently!'

'Yes, Mr Holmes. If you wants a bobby—I'll find you a bobby.' And with that he sprinted away.

'He's as sharp as a needle, and totally reliable, that one,' said Holmes, nodding in the direction of the rapidly disappearing figure. 'Now, Mr Bunyan—when was Mr Crosby last seen alive?'

'At supper last night,' replied the clergyman. 'Mrs Crosby told me that she ate supper with her husband at about eight o'clock.'

'And after that . . .?'

'He said he had some urgent work to finish, and went downstairs to his office in the bank chambers.'

'So,' muttered Holmes thoughtfully, 'he was alive shortly after eight o'clock last night. Watson, what would you say was the cause of death?'

'I've never seen a body in this condition before, Holmes—never. That makes it extremely difficult to answer your question. But as a guess—and it's only a guess—I would say that he died from the loss of blood. Of course, he may already have been dead at the time the blood was drained from his body, but there is no obvious wound or sign of assault.'

'You confirm my own observations, Watson.'

Sherlock Holmes took a magnifying lens from his coat pocket and began a closer examination of the corpse. 'Aha!' he cried triumphantly, after several minutes had passed. 'There is a wound, Watson—

admittedly a very small one—here upon the neck. Here, take my lens and see for yourself.'

Through the lens I could make out a small, round incision, smeared with dried, blackened blood. 'Remarkable,' I said. 'I've never seen anything like it.'

'Neither have I,' admitted Holmes. 'We are facing here an entirely new horror. The man or creature who did this to poor Crosby kills in a way I have never encountered before.'

'I have!' exclaimed Henry Bunyan. 'At least—in my readings in folklore I have come upon a creature capable of inflicting just such an injury, and causing just such a death.'

Holmes turned and looked at the clergyman, asking a question by raising an eyebrow as he did so.

'A vampire, Mr Holmes—a vampire! There are vampires in the folk tales of many countries, but especially eastern Europe and the Balkans; countries such as Albania, Hungary, and Romania. Can all these stories be mere superstition? Or is there something behind them? The state of poor Crosby's corpse seem to tell us that the folk tales are true—and that a vampire is now stalking the streets and back alleys of London.'

SHERLOCK HOLMES' TALES OF TERROR

Another body has been found that is drained of every last drop of blood. Inspector Lestrade of Scotland Yard is baffled.

Only Sherlock Holmes—the world's greatest detective—can solve this case. But Holmes himself has been attacked by the vampire creature and is lying close to death.

If Holmes dies there will be no one who can stop the world's greatest criminal mastermind—Dr Grimsby Defoe.

THE VAMPIRE SERPENT

#3

Coming to a bookstore near you!

Next in the series

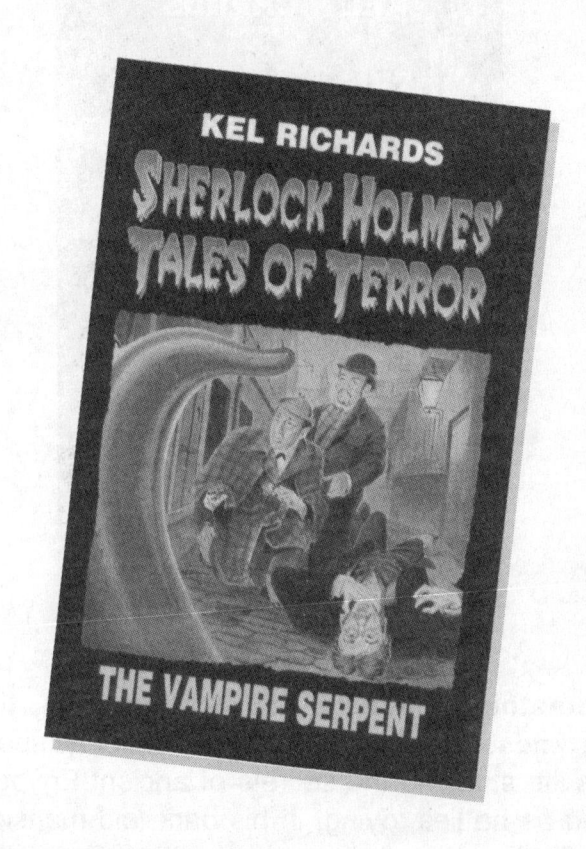

KEL RICHARDS

SHERLOCK HOLMES' TALES OF TERROR

THE VAMPIRE SERPENT

Don't miss it

KEL RICHARDS

SHERLOCK HOLMES' TALES OF TERROR

THE CURSE OF THE PHARAOHS

Something strange is walking in the darkness! Professor Soames Coffin has spent his life studying the secrets of ancient Egypt—and as he lies, dying, in his dark, old mansion in Scotland he believes the old magic of the Pharaohs will bring him back to life. Soon the creature who is The Walking Dead is stalking the living . . . including Sherlock Holmes!

The world of Ben Bartholomew is a world of standover gangs and armed terrorists, a world in which a private eye for hire must carry a gun if he wants to live beyond lunchtime. When Ben Bartholomew begins investigating, he finds that he has stumbled onto the ultimate locked-room mystery!

Guaranteed to be a can't-put-down book.

SHERLOCK HOLMES' TALES OF TERROR

by Kel Richards

#1	The Curse of the Pharaohs	6.95
#2	The Headless Monk	6.95
#3	The Vampire Serpent	6.95

Post me Sherlock Holmes' Tales of Terror NOW!

Available wherever you buy books, or use this order form.

Beacon Communication Pty Ltd
PO Box 1317
LANE COVE NSW 2066
Phone or Fax: (02) 9427 4197

Please send me the books I have ticked above. I am enclosing $_____ (please add $4.00 to cover postage and handling). Send cheque or money order. To use credit card phone for details.

Name _____

Address _____

_____ Pcode _____

Offer good in Australia only. Prices subject to change.